in the

Caves, deep in

the cliffs at the edge of

the Bay of Dolphins.

At the cave-mouths, the merfolk sit sunning themselves on the rocks. They are a magical mixture of humans and sea-creatures, with tails covered in beautiful, glowing, glinting scales. When merbabies are born, they are given an enchanted comb – it must never be lost. . .

Look out for Maddie's further adventures in Zavania. . .

Unicorn Wishes

Princess Wishes

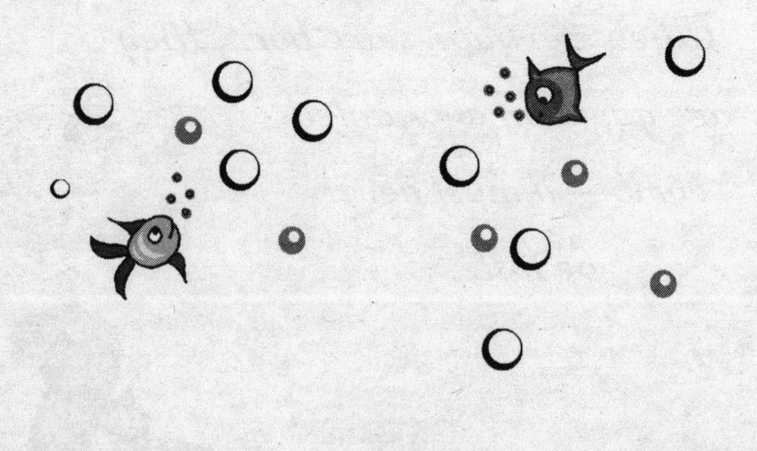

Mermaid Wishes

Carol Barton

Illustrated by Charlotte Alder

SCHOLASTIC

Scholastic Children's Books,
Euston House, 24 Eversholt Street
London NW1 1DB, UK
A division of Scholastic Ltd
London ~ New York ~Toronto ~ Sydney ~ Auckland
Mexico City ~ New Delhi ~ Hong Kong

First published in the UK by Scholastic Ltd, 1999
This edition published by Scholastic Ltd, 2006

10 digit ISBN 0 439 95100 3
13 digit ISBN 978 0 439 95100 5

Printed in the UK by CPI Bookmarque, Croydon, CR0 4TD

3 4 5 6 7 8 9 10

Contents

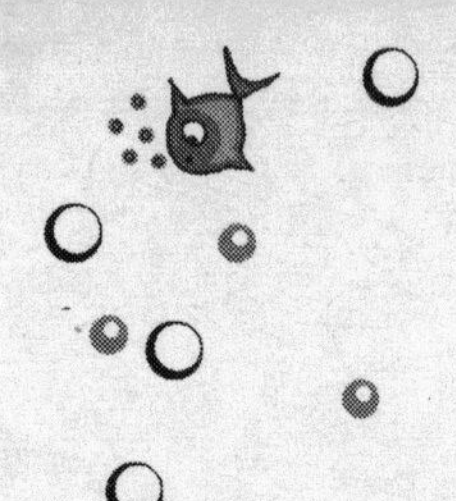

For Amy, with love.

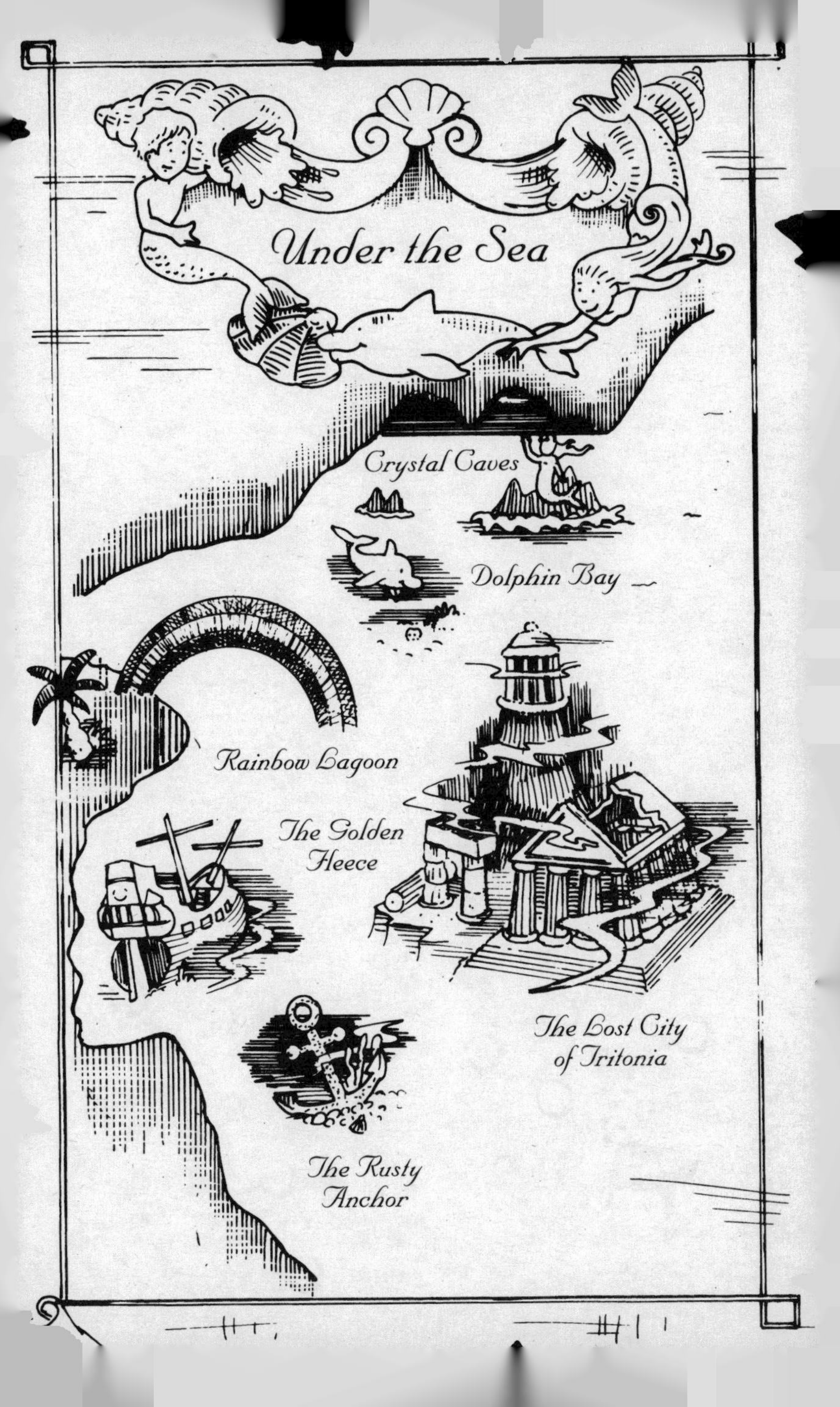
Under the Sea
Crystal Caves
Dolphin Bay
Rainbow Lagoon
The Golden Fleece
The Lost City of Tritonia
The Rusty Anchor

Chapter One

The Return of the Raven

"Maddie hasn't really got a boyfriend. She just wants us to think that."

"How could she have a boyfriend? Who would look at her?"

Muffled giggles broke out in the back of the classroom and Maddie O'Neill put her head down, her cheeks burning. Her friend Lucy, who was sitting beside her,

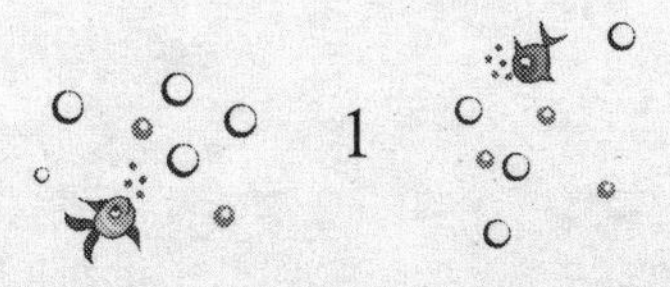

threw her a concerned glance. "Don't take any notice of them, Maddie," she whispered behind her hand.

Maddie shook her head. She was well used to the jeers of a certain little band in her class. Encouraged by Jessica Coatsworth, their ringleader, they took great delight in teasing her over her red hair, her freckles and the brace she had to wear on her teeth.

Today had been worse than most. It was the day of the school party and just before their teacher had arrived for lessons they had taunted Maddie over the fact that she would never, ever, have a boyfriend. At that she had rounded on them. "If you must know," she'd said hotly, "I already have a boyfriend – so there!"

When the lesson ended and their teacher left the room they crowded round

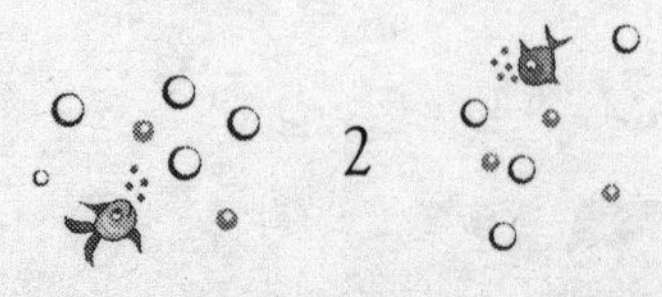

her desk, just as she'd known they would.

"So who is he then?" sneered Jessica. "Are you bringing him to the party tonight?"

"Is he good-looking?" demanded Emily Jackson, a tall skinny girl.

"He must have a problem with his eyesight," said someone else and they all shrieked with mirth.

"Well, Josh Bates has made sure I am going to be at the party," said Jessica, tossing back her long hair. "And I have a new cropped top and a pair of gold satin leggings to wear. What will you wear, Maddie?" She gave a spiteful little smile. "Something purple to clash with your hair and spotted to match your freckles?"

"Don't take any notice of them, Maddie," said Lucy, peering anxiously at her through her large round glasses.

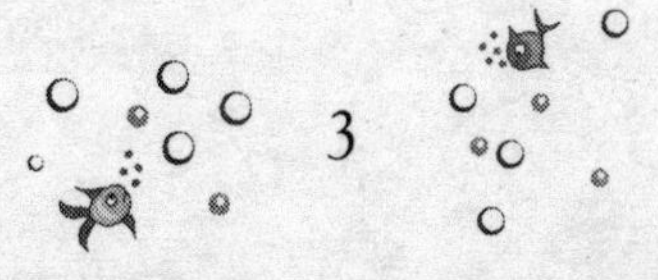

But Maddie was getting angry. Staring straight ahead, her eyes were bright and on her cheeks there were two vivid patches of colour.

"She made this boyfriend up," Jessica went on after a moment, "she must have done. He doesn't really exist—"

"Well, that's just where you're wrong!" Maddie spun round and faced the other girl, her eyes flashing now and her red curls bobbing furiously. "He does exist!"

"So who is he? What's his name?" taunted Jessica. "Come on, tell us."

"His name is Sebastian," said Maddie. As soon as the words left her lips she wished she'd kept quiet. All this time she'd kept him a secret, not even telling Lucy or her mother, and now here she was telling Jessica Coatsworth, of all people.

The laughter and jeering had died away

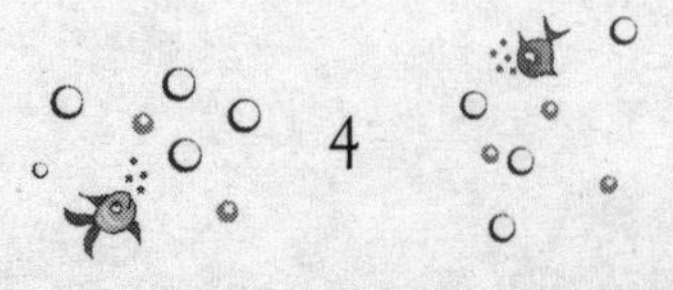

and in the silence that followed Maddie realized with a sinking heart that they were all staring at her.

"Se . . . *bast* . . . ian!" said Jessica, her lip curling contemptuously. "What sort of name is that?"

"So where does he live?" demanded Emily. "Come on, tell us!"

"She can't," said Jessica. "Because it's like we said. She's made him up!"

"Well, if *I* was going to make someone up," said another of the girls with a peal of laughter, "I wouldn't use a name like that. Honestly, I ask you. Sebastian! If that's not a made up name, I don't know what is. Now, if she said he was called James or Ben or something like that, we just might have believed her . . . but *Sebastian*!"

"I haven't made him up," said Maddie through gritted teeth. "His name *is*

Sebastian. He's older than me, at least two years older and he lives. . ." She paused. "He lives in . . . in another place."

"What do you mean?" demanded Jessica, her eyes narrowing suspiciously. "Another place? Do you mean abroad, another country?"

"Yes," said Maddie. "That's exactly what I mean. Another country. So he couldn't come to the party anyway."

"Huh," said Emily. She eyed her up and down, but not in quite the same way as before, this time with a sort of grudging interest. "So how often do you get to see him then?"

"Not too often," admitted Maddie. She didn't want to say she'd only seen him once because that would be sure to start them off again.

"So does he come to your house?" This

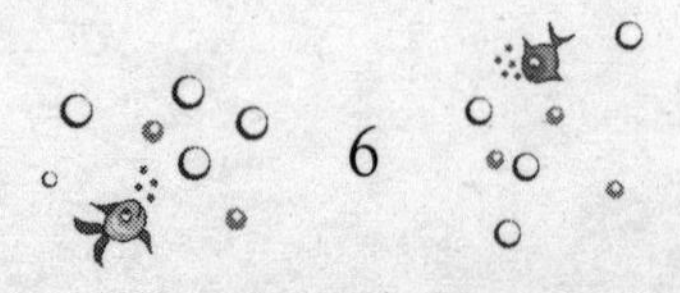

was from Lucy and even she sounded curious now.

"No." Maddie shook her head. "I . . . I went to his. . ."

They all stared at her in silence and desperately she wondered what to say next. She was already beginning to fear that she'd said far too much. She was saved, however, for at that moment another teacher came into the classroom to start a lesson.

"You didn't tell me about this boy, Sebastian," said Lucy as she and Maddie walked home together from school.

"I haven't really told anyone," said Maddie. "I didn't think anyone would believe me."

"I thought I was your friend." Lucy sounded hurt.

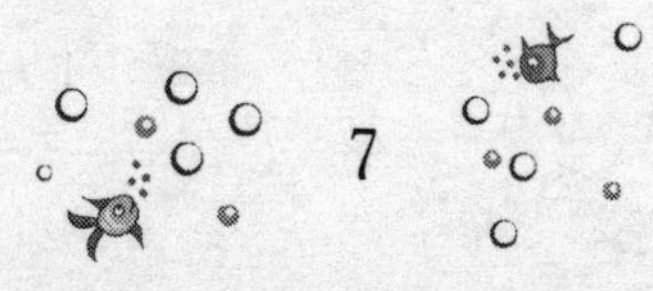

"Oh you are," said Maddie. "Of course you are, Lucy. You are the only one who is."

"Then you should have told me. I would have told you if I had got a boyfriend," said Lucy unhappily, as if she didn't really believe there was any chance of that. Then brightening up a little, she said, "So what's he like then?"

"Sebastian? Oh, he's nice," said Maddie. "Very nice. And actually he isn't really my boyfriend, I just said that to shut Jessica up. He's just a friend, but a special sort of friend if you know what I mean."

"So where did you meet him?" asked Lucy curiously.

"He was in his boat in the stream at the bottom of my garden," said Maddie. "He took me on a journey to meet his . . . his people."

"His people? You mean his family?"

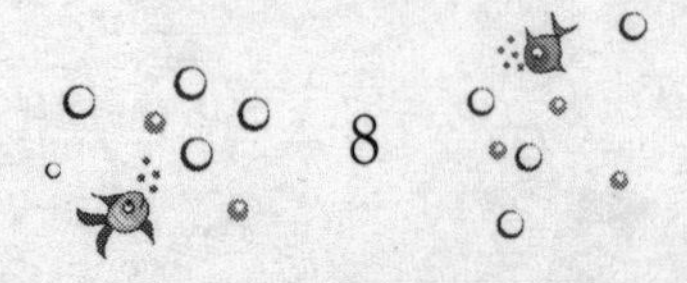

"Not exactly." Maddie hesitated. "He doesn't have any parents. He lives with a man called Zenith who is . . . well, his sort of boss, and a lady called Thirza who looks after them both, you know, does the cooking and everything."

"What funny names," said Lucy. "Sebastian, and Zenith, and now Thirza. I suppose they sound funny because they are foreign . . . because they live in another country."

"Yes." Maddie nodded. "I suppose so."

They walked on in silence for a while then, just as they neared the end of Maddie's road where Lucy would turn off to go to her own house, she said, "So where is it, this other country? What's it called?"

"It's called Zavania," said Maddie. "And it's a long way down river." She hesitated

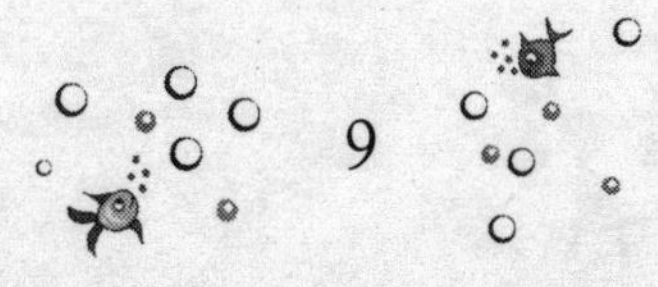

again, not sure how much she should tell even Lucy. "It's a strange place," she added at last.

"What do you mean, strange?" asked Lucy.

"Well, it seems anything can happen in Zavania . . . it's like a magic place."

"Wow," said Lucy. "Sounds like fun."

"Oh, it is," said Maddie. "It is."

"Are you going again?"

"I hope so," she replied. "Sebastian said he'd come and get me again."

"Cool," said Lucy. "Doesn't your mum mind you going?"

"Er no, not really." Maddie couldn't quite bring herself to say that her mum didn't even know she'd been.

"Lucky old you," said Lucy. "My mum would never let me do anything like that. Oh well, I suppose I'd better go and get

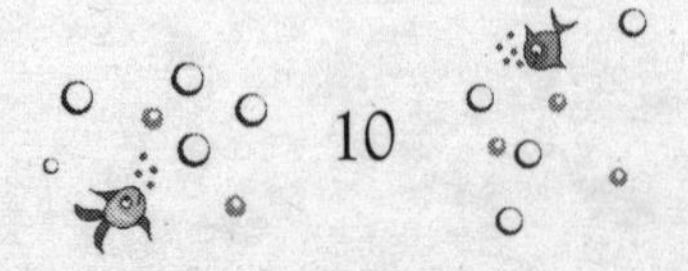

changed for the party. See you later, Maddie."

"Yes, Lucy," Maddie replied. "See you later." She watched as her friend walked off down her own road swinging her school bag. How could she have told Lucy that there was a good chance her own mother wouldn't have let her go to Zavania either, if she'd known? But how could she explain that it hadn't been like that? That she hadn't deliberately defied her mother, that the trip to Zavania had simply happened, and that when she had returned home, almost no time at all seemed to have passed and her mother hadn't even suspected she'd been gone.

She sighed and began to walk slowly down the road to her own house. But it hadn't only been the time that had been strange. It had all been strange. How

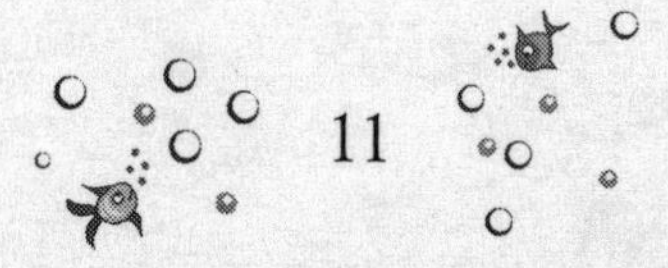

could she even begin to tell anyone, even Lucy, of the things she had seen in that strange land where time stood still?

Where would she start? How could she expect them to believe that Sebastian's friend and protector was a huge black raven, not just any old raven, but one who was called Zak and who could talk, and that his boss, the man Zenith, was actually a magician who granted people's wishes?

No one would believe that. Not even Lucy. And if Maddie herself was completely honest, she had to admit there were still times when she wondered if she hadn't dreamed the whole thing.

Six weeks had passed. Six long weeks. She had lost count of the number of times she'd gone down the garden to the stream to see if Sebastian's boat was there, moored beneath the willows where it had

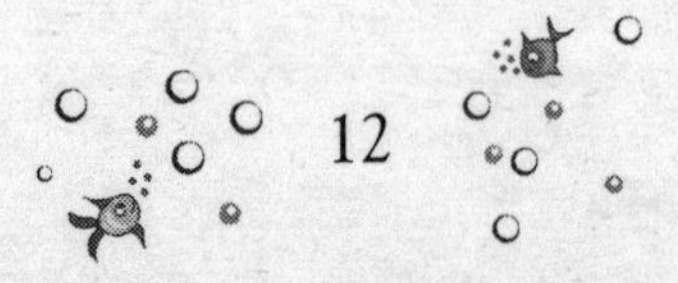

been before. But every time the stream was empty, without even so much as a ripple to suggest the presence of a boat.

Once, in desperation, she had even

walked down the bank of the stream to the point where it joined the wider, faster-flowing river, a place where she was forbidden to go, but it all looked so different from that time she had made the journey in the boat with Sebastian. Then the fields on either side had been filled with flowers and the sky had been a startling blue, but now there were only muddy banks and the odd jetty or landing stage amongst the reeds.

She had believed he would come back, even Zak had said there would be another time, but as one day had followed another, Maddie had begun to despair.

And now, she wished that she hadn't let Jessica Coatsworth and the others goad her into telling about Sebastian, for until that moment she had been determined to keep him a secret. Something had just

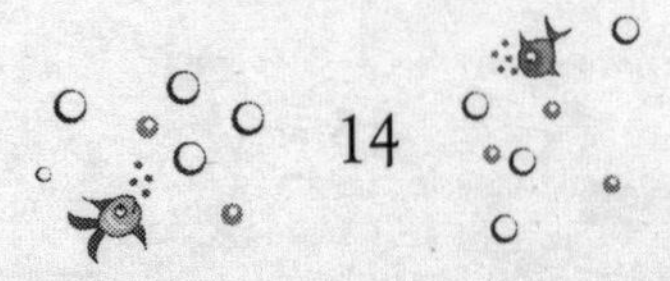

snapped inside when they had gone on and on at her.

When she reached her house she went round to the back and opened the door. Her mother was in the kitchen.

"Hello, Maddie," she said. "Had a good day?"

Maddie mumbled a reply as she helped herself to orange juice and biscuits. She never told her mother about the teasing these days. She was afraid that if she did her mother would go to the school to try to sort things out. Maddie feared that would only make Jessica and the others even worse.

"I'm going up to my room," she said.

"You'd better get your homework done so that you can get ready for the party, Maddie," her mother said as she opened the oven and popped a casserole inside.

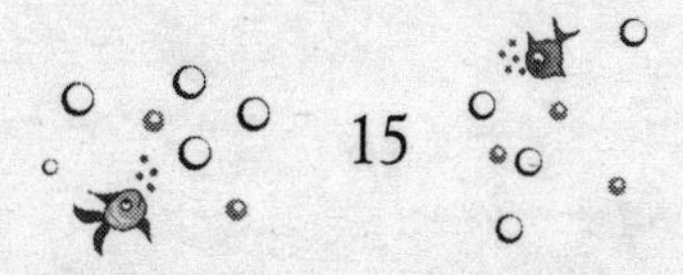

"I've ironed your turquoise top and skirt."

"Do I have to go?" said Maddie. "I don't really want to."

"Oh, Maddie," said her mother. "I've made some fairy cakes for you to take and a plateful of cheese and cress sandwiches. Besides, I think you should, and Lucy will be disappointed if you don't, won't she?"

"Yes," Maddie sighed. "I suppose she will."

"Well, you've got about an hour before you need to go."

Maddie nodded, went out into the hall and, munching her biscuit, began to climb the stairs. In her room she dumped her school bag on the floor then stood for a moment before the window, watching as her mother threw a handful of crusts on to the lawn for the birds before disappearing back inside the house.

The birds swooped down as soon as she had gone, starlings scrapping and jostling each other, twittering sparrows, and a group of rooks who flapped and strutted, trying to frighten off the smaller birds.

Maddie smiled at their antics and was about to turn away from the window, when suddenly she stopped as something caught her attention.

She realized now that one of the birds which she had first thought to be a rook was much larger than the others. It swooped and dived, coming closer to the house than the other birds.

Maddie stiffened and leaned forward, taking hold of the windowsill. The bird swooped again, this time coming in close to her bedroom window.

There was something very different

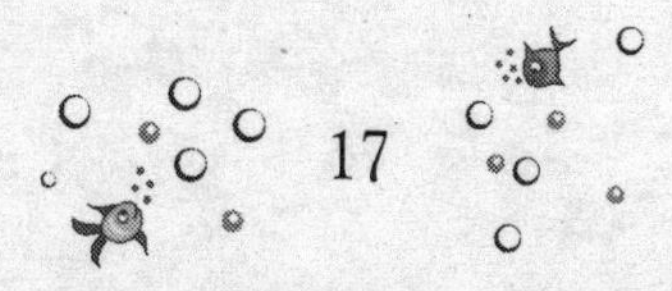

about this bird. Maddie's heart gave a great lurch of excitement.

Could it be?

Was it Zak, the raven?

As the bird disappeared from her view she turned from the window and ran out of the room and down the stairs. Luckily her mother had come out of the kitchen and was in the living-room talking to someone on the telephone, so Maddie was able to let herself out of the back door without being noticed.

The birds on the lawn rose in a great mass, flapping and squawking at being disturbed.

All except one. One great black bird who perched on the roof of the garden shed and eyed her up and down.

Slowly, cautiously, her heart thumping, Maddie moved forward. "Zak?" she whispered. "Is it you?"

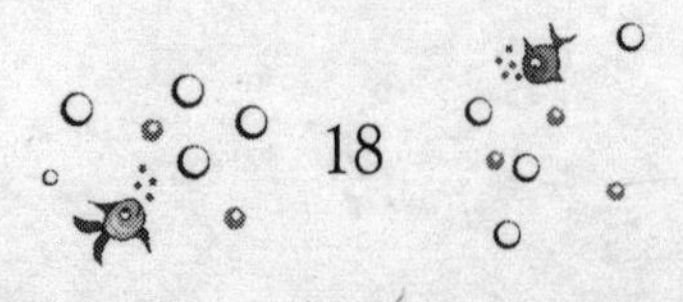

The bird blinked then flapped its great wings once before rising slowly into the air, hovering there as if it was waiting for Maddie to follow.

Hardly daring to breathe she moved forward as the great bird flapped its wings majestically again, then flying low led the way right down past the flower borders and through her dad's vegetable plot to the trees at the bottom of the garden. Then it disappeared from sight beneath the drooping branches of the willows.

"Oh," Maddie gasped, as she ran stumbling over cabbage stalks in her effort to keep up. "Please wait!"

When at last she reached the willows and parted the branches she peered anxiously from left to right.

All was still and at first she couldn't see anything, then turning her head she saw

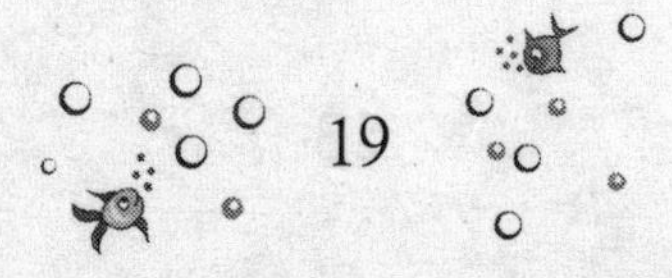

the bird. He was perched on a log and was watching her.

"Zak?" she said uncertainly. "Is it you?"

"Of course it's me." The bird flapped his wings. "Who did you think it was, for goodness' sake!"

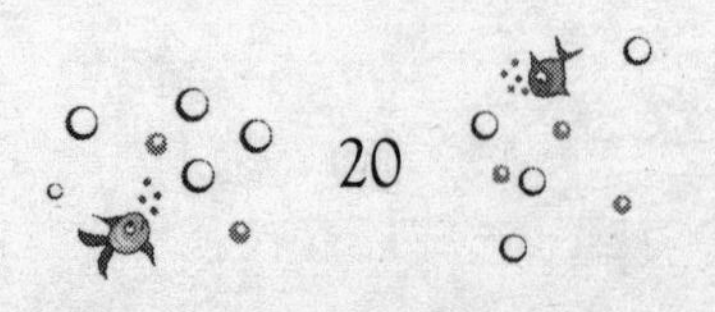

Chapter Two

Into Zavania

"Oh, Zak, it *is* you!" Maddie clasped her hands together. "I thought it was, but I'd almost given up hope. It's been such a long time."

"Has it?" said Zak. "Days fly by as far as I'm concerned. It's all go. Never a moment's peace."

"Is Sebastian with you?" As Maddie looked

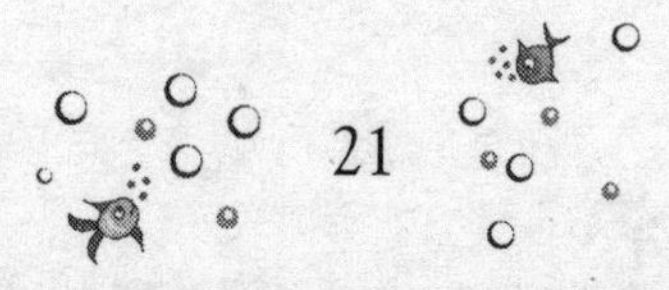

round and peered beneath the willows at the stream she found she was holding her breath. And then, even as she watched, she saw a slight movement in the water and silently the end of the boat slid into view.

And suddenly there he was, just like before, standing proud and aloof at the far end of the boat with the pole in his hands. His black cloak was flung over one shoulder, revealing his loose white shirt with its tightened cuffs and the black breeches that ended at the knee.

"Sebastian!" she cried.

He looked up then and saw her on the bank of the stream, peering down at him through the leaves of the willows. "Hello Maddie," he said, and a little colour flushed his cheeks.

"Oh, I knew you'd come back," Maddie cried.

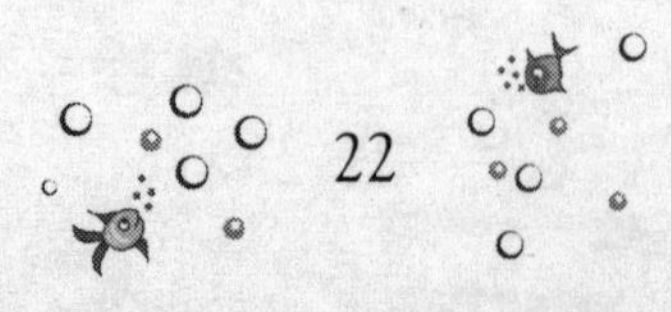

"I had to wait for someone to make a wish," said Sebastian, manoeuvring the boat alongside the bank and holding out his hand to help her step aboard.

"And hasn't anyone made a wish until now?" asked Maddie.

"Oh, there have been plenty of wishes," said Zak, flapping his wings again before perching on the end of the pole. "Ten a penny, but none important enough for Zenith to pronounce them Official Wishes."

"So has someone made an important wish now?" asked Maddie, as she sat down in the midst of the heap of brightly coloured cushions at the bottom of the boat.

"Yes," Sebastian replied, turning as he spoke to push the boat away from the bank again. "But we don't know who it is yet. We have to wait for Zenith the WishMaster to tell us."

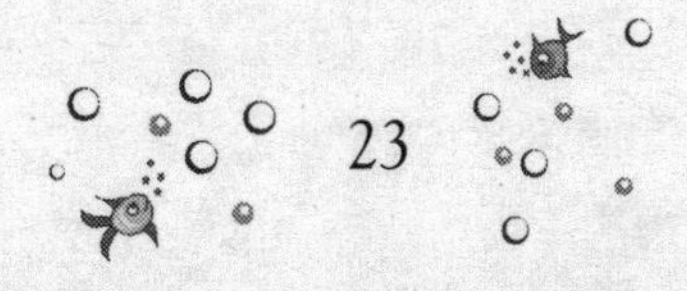

"So did he say I could help?" asked Maddie, as she recalled the fuss there had been the last time trying to persuade the WishMaster to let her accompany Sebastian on his wish-granting mission.

It was Zak who answered her question. With a loud throaty chuckle he said, "Not only has he said you can go, he ordered us to come and fetch you."

"Did he?" Maddie's eyes widened in amazement.

Zak laughed again. "Yes," he replied. "There was poor old Sebastian summoning up the courage to ask Zenith if he could come and get you and Zenith beat him to it. He said, and I quote, 'Sebastian has the tendency to get carried away by the strength of his magic powers.' And that you, Maddie, are 'a steadying influence upon him'."

"Zenith said that!" Maddie's eyes grew even larger.

"I must say I'm inclined to agree with him," said Zak. "And you're jolly useful when it comes to learning the spells. Sebastian's memory doesn't get a lot better, no matter how much magic he performs."

"I can't help it if I forget lines," muttered Sebastian from the rear of the boat.

Sensing tension between the two friends, Maddie decided to change the subject. "I only have about an hour," she said. "I have to go to a school party. I don't really want to go but Mum says I have to, so I must be back in time."

"No problem," said Sebastian. "You will be home at the exact time you need to be."

Maddie sighed and wriggled further down in the cushions, making herself more

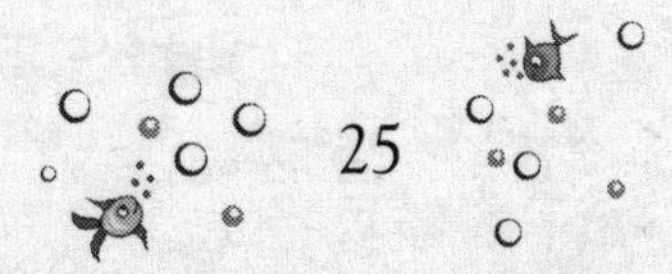

comfortable as the boat began its journey into Zavania.

While they had been talking they had moved through the tunnel of willows, out into a curtain of mist that snaked and curled around them in wraith-like strands. Then finally they burst through the mist into bright sunlight that danced and sparkled on the water.

It was just as it had been before on that first occasion when Maddie had made the journey. Once again, the fields on either side of the river were filled with wild flowers, the sky was an endless blue and brightly coloured fish leapt and darted alongside the boat. Dark forests of fir-trees rose in the distance against a backdrop of purple mountains whose snow-covered pinnacles soared into the sky.

But more comforting to Maddie than all

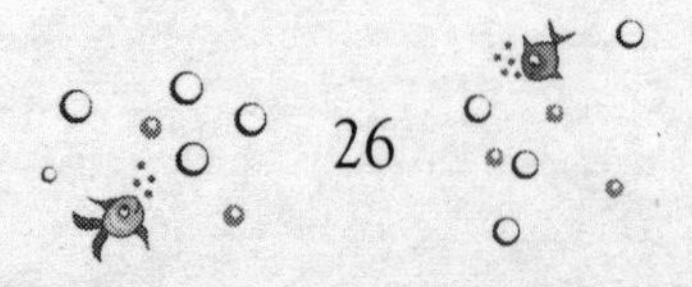

that was the fact that the tall handsome boy with the golden skin and almond-shaped eyes who stood at the end of the boat was real and not just a dream character or a figure from her imagination. He was real, just as the raven, Zak, was real, and they had come back for her because they needed her.

They seemed to complete the journey in an incredibly short space of time and, almost before Maddie knew it, they were in the stream in the gardens of Zavania's royal castle and Sebastian and Zak were tying up the boat at the small wooden jetty.

As they left the jetty and hurried over the small rustic bridge towards the castle, Maddie glanced around her. She half expected to see the Princess Lyra and found herself dreading the prospect. The

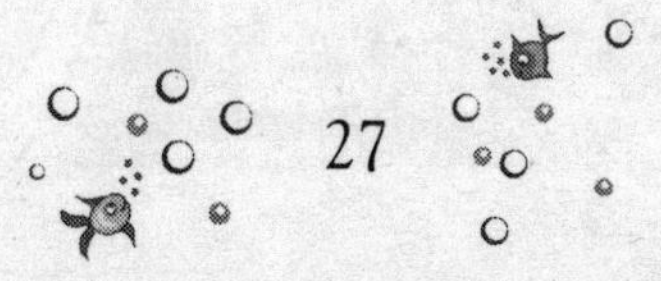

princess had taken an obvious dislike to Maddie the last time she had visited Zavania and had seemed to resent her friendship with Sebastian, but today, mercifully, there was no sign of her.

Maddie would have liked to linger in the garden, for it was a truly magical place with fountains of raspberry-flavoured water and the most weird but beautiful flowers she'd ever seen, but Sebastian hurried her on.

"You know how Zenith hates to be kept waiting," he said.

"Yes, for goodness' sake hurry up," squawked Zak, flying low alongside them as they approached the castle, "I don't fancy being turned into a worm, which is what Zenith threatened me with the last time I was late. Just imagine, me as a worm!"

"You'd probably have made a nice meal

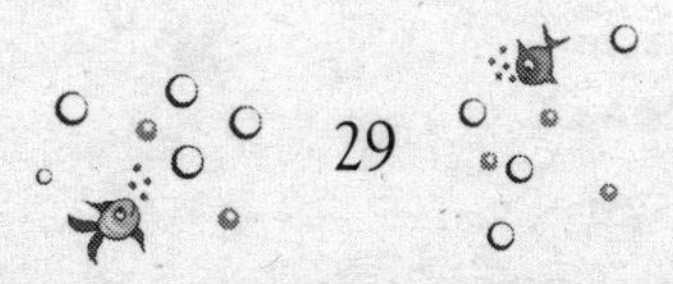

for the castle jackdaws," said Sebastian with a laugh.

"What?" spluttered Zak. "Those pesky jackdaws don't deserve anything, let alone. . ."

But Sebastian wasn't listening for by now they had reached the East Tower, his home and that of Zenith, the WishMaster. As they approached the entrance the door was flung open and a tiny woman, with a skin like a wrinkled walnut and black button eyes, stood there with her hands on her hips.

"Oh," gasped Maddie, out of breath now from running. "It's Thirza!"

"What time do you call this!" snapped Thirza in her high-pitched, bell-like voice.

"We got here as soon as we could." Sebastian paused for a moment, hands on his thighs as he regained his breath.

"Well, you'd better go straight on up while I get a drink for Maddie. He's stamping about up there. Go on with you. Get a move on." Thirza stood aside as Sebastian went past her and began to climb the steps to the turret room, then as he disappeared from their sight she turned to Maddie.

"Come on," she said, just as if she'd only seen her a few moments before. "Come and have a goblet of my strawberry cordial."

"Oh, thank you." Maddie had tasted the cordial before and knew how delicious it was. She followed Thirza into the tower where they climbed up the steps to the first floor. Zak streaked past them and was perched on his rail waiting for them when they arrived.

"So," said Thirza a little later, when

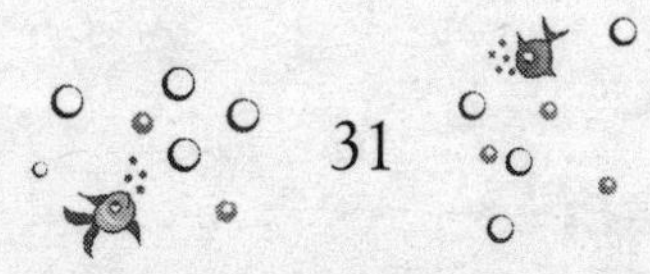

Maddie was seated at the long, highly-polished table sipping her drink, "Zenith has sent for you. You must have impressed him the last time. I've never known him to send for anyone from the Other Place before."

"Sebastian wanted me to come as well," said Maddie.

"Well yes, that goes without saying," said Thirza with a sniff. "His head can be turned by a pretty face . . . but Zenith, that's a different matter altogether."

"But I haven't got a pretty face." Maddie lowered her goblet and stared at Thirza.

"Who says you haven't?" demanded Thirza.

"Everybody," said Maddie. "The girls at school, especially Jessica Coatsworth, they make fun of me all the time."

As she spoke there came the sound of an

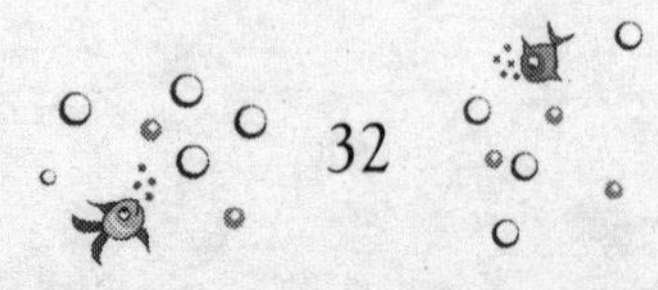

angry squawk from Zak's corner and she turned to look at him. Then, as the raven began strutting up and down along his perch, she added gloomily, "Mind you, I suppose you can't wonder at it really, not with this awful hair of mine . . . and my freckles . . . and this dreadful brace on my teeth."

"Take no notice of them," snapped Thirza. "You'll have the last laugh one day, my girl, just you wait and see."

Maddie doubted that what Thirza said could ever happen, but she had no further time to think about it, for at that moment Sebastian appeared again on the stairs and beckoned furiously to her.

"I have to go, Thirza." Jumping to her feet Maddie set down the goblet and ran across to the stairs. Once again the raven swooped past her and preceded both her

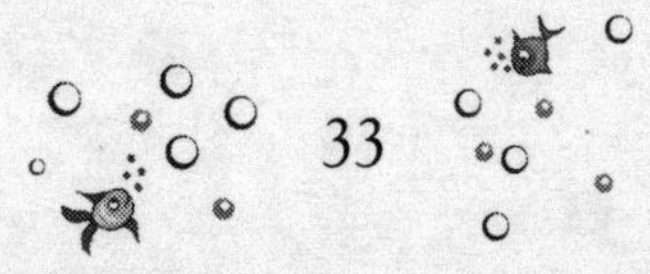

and Sebastian as they climbed up to the turret room.

The first time Maddie had entered the WishMaster's room she had been terrified, and the sight of all the instruments and potions had done little to calm her nerves. This time it was different, although she was still in awe of the great man, she wasn't really afraid of him, and when she finally stood before him she even managed a smile.

"Madeleine," he boomed, as he stood there, his bald head gleaming in the glow from the dozens of candles that lit the turret room, his dark cloak wrapped around him, and his black eyebrows meeting in a ferocious frown.

"Maddie," she corrected.

"Quite," he muttered gruffly, "Maddie. So are you ready, girl, to join this wretched boy on another assignment?"

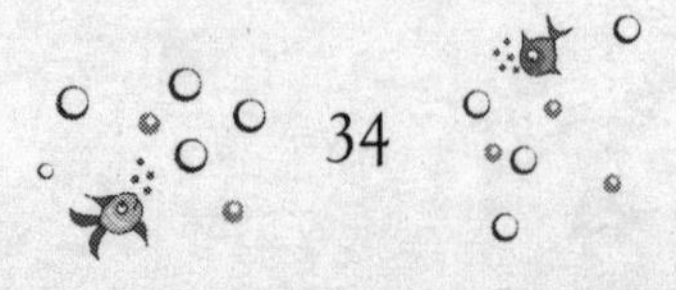

"Oh yes," said Maddie. "Quite ready."

"So the Ice Queen didn't put you off the last time with all her shenanigans?"

"No." Maddie gulped, shaking her head. Then remembering how frightened she had been when they had been in the clutches of the evil Ice Queen, she added anxiously, "Well, not too much . . . but it won't be anything to do with her again, will it?"

Zak gave a squawk and hid his head under his wing and even Sebastian paled at the awful prospect.

"What if it was her?" asked Zenith. "Would you still want to help?"

Maddie gulped. "Yes," she said, but her voice came out like one of Zak's croaks.

"Well, that's very commendable of you, I'm sure," said Zenith. Then with a glance at them all, he went on, "But no, it isn't anything to do with her this time."

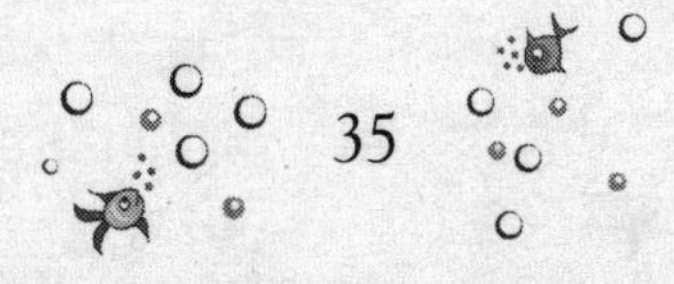

They all breathed a sigh of relief.

"She hasn't had time to get herself together again," Zenith went on, "although I doubt we've heard the last of her, but no . . . this assignment is something quite different."

"So who has made the wish?" asked Sebastian.

There was silence in the turret room for a moment as they all waited expectantly to hear what Zenith had to say.

"It is a mermaid," said the WishMaster at last, when he knew he had their full attention. "A mermaid called Seraphina, who lives in the Crystal Caves on the far side of the Bay of Dolphins."

"And her wish?" asked Maddie.

"Her wish," said Zenith, "is that her comb, which has been stolen, should be returned to her."

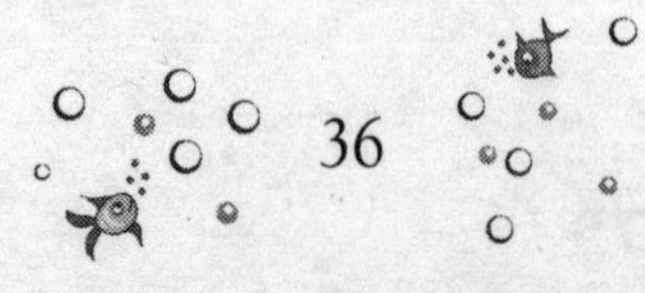

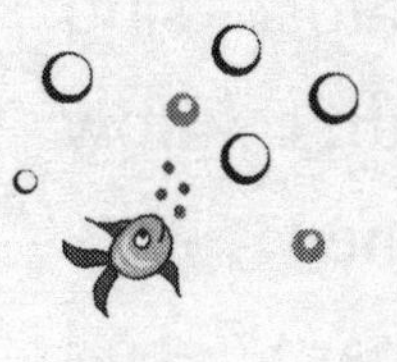

Chapter Three

Dolphin Bay

"I can't see why that should be so important," said Maddie, before she could stop herself. Then when Zenith paused and glowered at her from under his eyebrows, she swallowed, but went on. "What I mean is, if her comb has been stolen, couldn't she just buy another one?"

"Oh boy!" croaked Zak from his corner of the turret room. "She obviously doesn't know anything about merfolk. . ."

"Merfolk?" Maddie interrupted in bewilderment. "Whatever are they?"

"Merfolk," said Sebastian, "refers to them both – mermaids and mermen."

"Well, I've heard of mermaids," said Maddie, "but I certainly didn't know there was such a thing as mermen. . ."

"Boy, has she got a lot to learn," said Zak sadly, shaking his head.

"Tell her, Sebastian, about merfolk and their combs," said Zenith wearily, pressing the back of his wrist to his forehead and turning away.

"A merchild," explained Sebastian patiently, "only ever has one comb. It is given to the child by its mother. This comb is the only one the child can

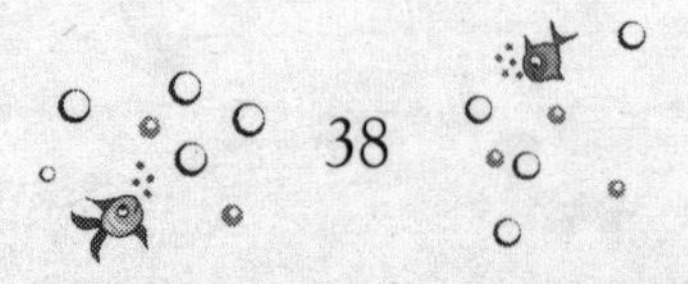

ever use to comb its hair which, if it isn't combed three times a day, becomes hopelessly tangled . . . so tangled, in fact, that it becomes matted and prevents the merchild from being able to swim. Isn't that right, Zenith?" Sebastian threw the WishMaster a questioning glance.

"Absolutely!" As Zenith turned back to them again the light from the candles caught the single gold hoop he wore in his ear. "So maybe now, girl," he went on, "you can see the importance of this, and why I have decided that it should be an Official Wish."

"Oh yes," said Maddie. "Yes, of course I do. I know how awful it is when my hair gets tangled and mine isn't particularly long. I've seen pictures of mermaids and they have very long hair. So where do we

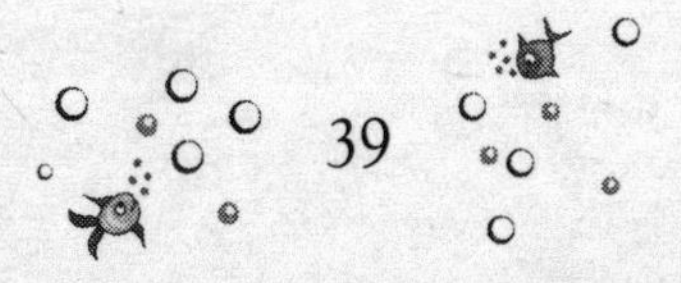

have to go? Where did you say this mermaid lives?"

"In the Crystal Caves on the far side of Dolphin Bay," said Zenith. "It was a dolphin who swam up the stream to the castle and told me the whole sad story. It seems that if Seraphina or indeed any other merperson can't swim, they would just wither away and die."

"Oh dear," said Zak, "we can't have that."

"Quite," said Zenith. "So your mission is to find out who stole the comb, to retrieve it, and to return it to the mermaid."

"Do we have any idea who might have taken it?" asked Sebastian dubiously.

"There have been several suggestions, according to the dolphin," said Zenith. "The stingrays and the devil fish have

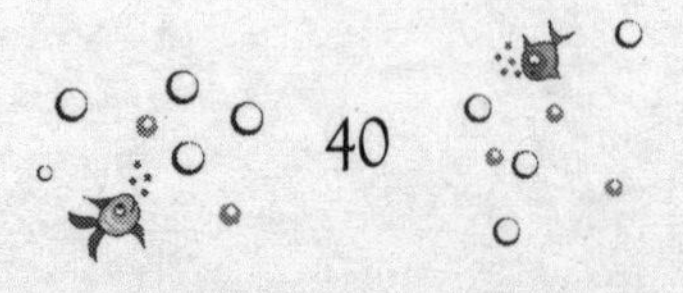

been causing trouble again recently, the barracudas are forever up to their tricks, and there's a band of prawns who have been thieving in that area—"

"All sounds a bit fishy to me," cackled Zak. "And wet," he added. "I don't like the water, it makes my feathers go spiky. I think if it's all the same to the rest of you, I'll give this one a miss."

Maddie threw him a startled glance. To go without Zak was unthinkable.

"You'll do no such thing," Zenith answered promptly, to her relief. "You'll go with them. They may be glad of your help."

Zak drew his head back between his wings and Maddie knew he was sulking.

"The rules are the same as always," said Zenith, moving to the cupboard on the

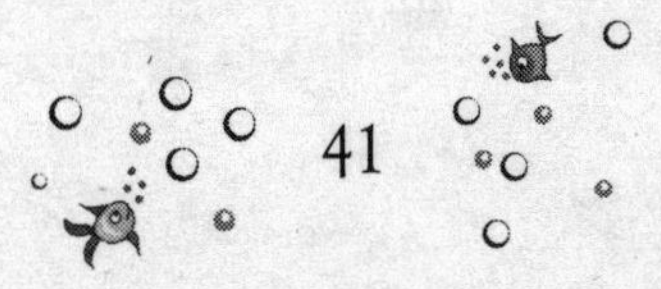

wall and unlocking it. "You have two spells to help you to grant the wish. These, you must memorize."

Ignoring Sebastian's groan he went on, "It is up to Sebastian how and when he chooses to use the spells, but he has me to answer to afterwards, and I shall be the judge of whether or not his choices were wise ones."

The WishMaster paused, and turning from the cupboard he threw Sebastian a stern glance. "Your choices, of course, will have a bearing on just when you will gain your Golden Spurs and become a fully-fledged WishMaster."

Sebastian swallowed and Zenith turned back to the cupboard.

"The one thing you must never forget," he went on, as he drew two scrolls of parchment and a black casket out of

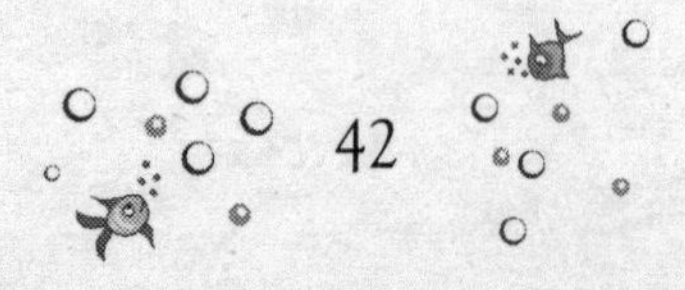

the cupboard, "is that once the spells have been used, you are on your own and not even my magic can come to your rescue."

He paused again and there was a deep silence in the turret room. Maddie found herself holding her breath as Zenith opened the casket.

"Here," he said, "is your conductor of magic." Out of the casket he drew a ring whose stone caught the light in a turquoise flash.

Sebastian stepped forward and the WishMaster slipped the ring on to his finger.

"It's beautiful," Maddie breathed.

"The stone is an aquamarine," said Zenith. "Very apt for an underwater adventure."

"As if I needed reminding!" The sound

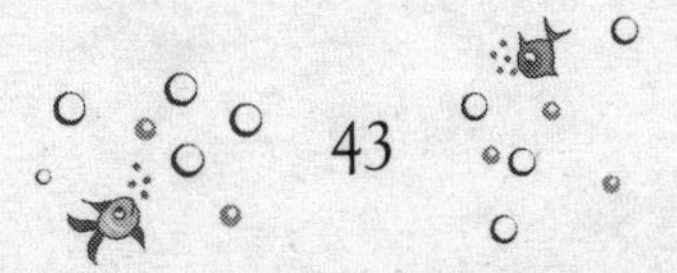

of a groan filled the air as Zak once again realized that he would be getting wet.

"And now," ignoring Zak, Zenith drew himself up to his full height, flicked back his cloak and with a flourish began to unroll one of the scrolls, "I will tell you the first of the spells. As you know, these scrolls can never, ever leave this room, so it is up to you to learn them as thoroughly as you can."

At last they were on their way and after bidding farewell to Thirza, who came to the landing jetty to wave them off, they were very soon moving swiftly downstream towards the sea.

"I'm sure I won't remember the spells," said Sebastian. "Each one that Zenith gives us seems to be worse than the one before."

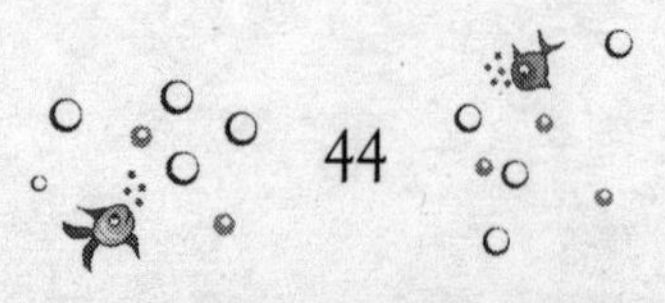

"Let's say them again," said Maddie. "Come on, all together, it's the only way to learn them, to keep repeating them. You too, Zak," she said sternly as the raven turned his back on them.

"Zak!"

"Oh, all right!" he squawked.

Maddie took a deep breath and hesitantly she began to recite the first of the spells.

"Zallaria Zallaria Zalliski,
By the power of the mighty
Zapphire.
Zaconda Zaconda Zarioka,
Send us the Turquoise Fire!"

"There you are, what was wrong with that?" demanded Maddie, looking at the other two. "That was quite easy."

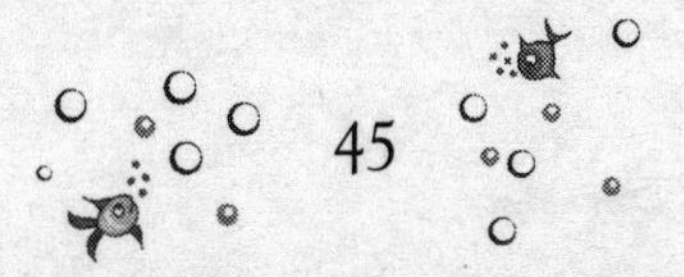

"I get them all muddled up," said Sebastian gloomily. "They all sound the same to me."

"But they aren't," cried Maddie. "They are all quite different. Now, come on, we'll try it again, and this time I don't want to say it on my own."

Amidst much muttering and grumbling Sebastian and Zak joined Maddie as together they repeated the lines of the first spell.

"Not bad," said Maddie when they had finished. "But you need to practise it. It has to be word perfect, Sebastian, you know that, otherwise it won't work. And what good would that be? You tell me. Just supposing that spell hadn't worked when we were trying to escape from the Ice Queen. Where would we be now, that's what I'd like to know!"

"Yeah, yeah, yeah, all right! We know. No need to keep on about it!" muttered Zak.

"Right. Well then," said Maddie, her eyes flashing, "just as long as you do know. So, let's have it again then.

"Zallaria Zallaria Zalliski. . ."

They sped on down the river and the air grew fresher and fresher.

"Look at those birds," said Sebastian pausing for a moment and resting on the pole. "They are seagulls – see how they swoop and dive."

"Conceited lot, seagulls," sniffed Zak. "Always showing off."

"It means we must be getting near the sea," said Sebastian and there was no mistaking the excitement in his voice.

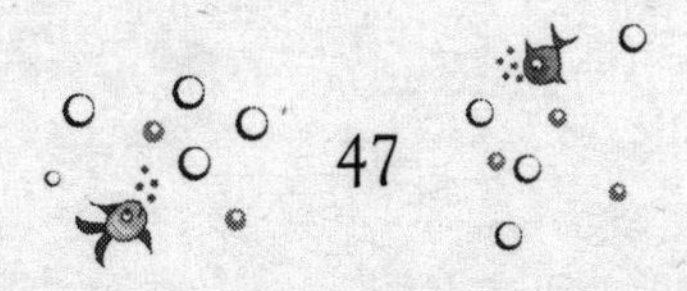

"In that case," said Maddie firmly, "it's high time we practised the second spell. Sebastian! Zak!" she said sharply when neither of them took any notice of her.

"Oh, all right," sighed Sebastian. "If we have to."

"Yes," said Maddie. "We do have to."

"Zambazine of Zizabar,
Zazcalooza Zazcalash.
Summon your blue magic
In one stupendous flash."

"Well," said Sebastian when they had finished, "I have to say, that one seems a bit easier. . . Oh, I say!" he exclaimed. Then, craning his neck, he said, "Look! There it is – there's the sea!"

"Oh," said Maddie, clasping her hands

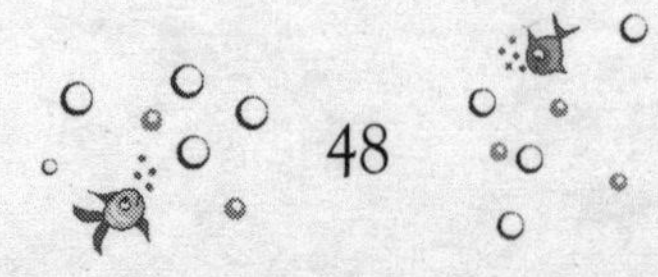

together. "It's so blue! I don't remember the sea being as blue as that."

"Well, I hope you can swim, that's all I can say," grumbled Zak.

"Oh yes," said Maddie. "I can swim, I learnt to swim in the pool at school."

"I learnt to swim in the river," said Sebastian. "What about you, Zak? I don't remember ever seeing you in the water."

"I don't go in the water any more than I can help." Zak flapped his wings. "Like I said, it makes my feathers go spiky."

"But can you swim?" asked Maddie anxiously.

"Let's put it this way," said Zak, "I won't drown."

By this time the river had opened out and joined the sea and Sebastian drew the boat into one side, on to a strip of

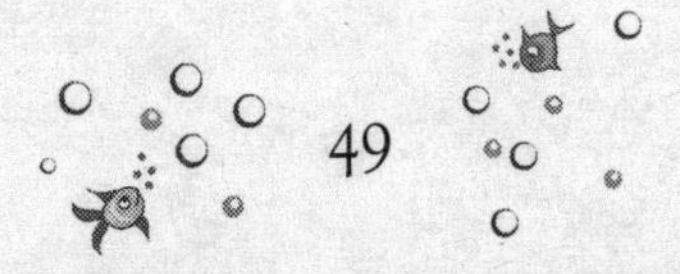

sandy beach strewn with dozens of shells and strands of coloured seaweed.

Shading his eyes from the bright sunlight Sebastian gazed across the sea.

"So where exactly are the Crystal Caves?" asked Maddie.

"According to Zenith they are on the far side of the bay. Look, over there, you can just see a line of cliffs." Sebastian pointed. "That must be where the caves are, where the merfolk live."

"How exciting," said Maddie. "I can't wait to see a real live mermaid."

"All this chatter is all very well," said Zak, who had been strutting up and down on the beach but who now turned and glared at the other two. "But how do you propose to get across the bay?"

"We have the boat. . ." Maddie began.

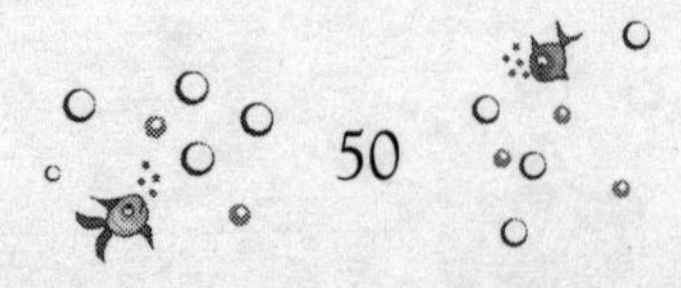

"Huh!" said Zak. "We wouldn't get very far in that. The pole might reach the bed of the river but there's no way it's going to be any good in the sea."

"Oh dear," said Maddie. "I hadn't thought of that."

"No," said Zak, "you were too busy making us recite those silly rhymes, that's why."

"There has to be a way," said Sebastian, gazing out to sea.

"It could well be that one of those silly rhymes, as you call them, might be our only means of crossing the bay," said Maddie coldly.

"I don't want to use a spell yet," said Sebastian. "It's far too soon."

"So do you have a better idea?" said Zak with a cackle.

"I think. . ." said Sebastian slowly. "I

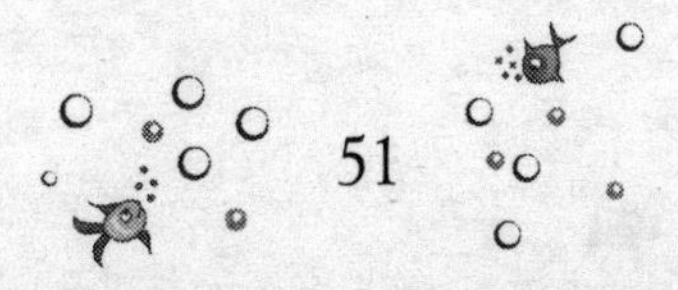

think I just might. Look, do you see that out there in the bay?"

"What?" Maddie screwed up her eyes against the sunlight, and far out in the bay she could see something leaping and playing above the waves. "Oh yes, what is it?"

"It's a dolphin," said Sebastian. "The bay is full of them! That must be how it got its name."

"You're quick," said Zak.

"I think they might be able to help us," said Sebastian, glaring at Zak. "I want you to fly out and ask them."

"Me?" squawked Zak indignantly.

"Yes, you," said Sebastian calmly. "But if it's too much for you, I'll ask the seagulls to do it for us."

"OK, OK, I'll go," said Zak with a huge sigh. Flapping his wings he took off, and

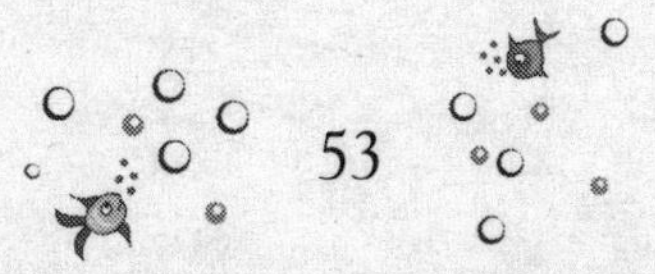

Maddie and Sebastian watched from the beach as he flew out across the bay.

"Do you think they will help us?" asked Maddie anxiously as they waited.

"If they can," said Sebastian. "They are very helpful creatures, dolphins, and don't forget it was a dolphin who first swam up river and told Zenith about the mermaid's wish. Zenith told me the Princess Lyra wanted to keep the dolphin when she saw it but he wouldn't let her."

"She would," said Maddie. They were silent for a while, then throwing Sebastian a quick glance, she said. "Has the princess been causing any more trouble since the last time I was here?"

"Not really," Sebastian chuckled. "I think she might have learnt her lesson, at least for a little while. She's away at the moment," he added.

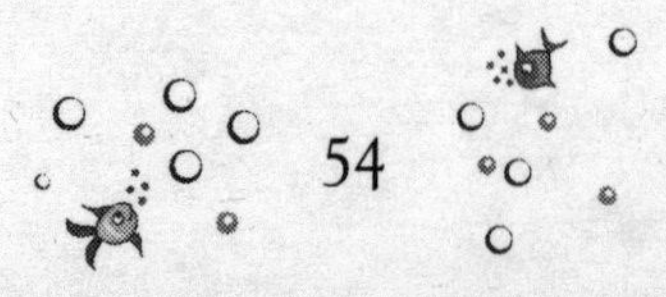

"Is she?" said Maddie.

"Yes, her parents have taken her and her brother to see the queen's sister."

Maddie didn't answer but she was relieved. Ever since her return to Zavania she had been dreading another encounter with the princess, who had made it quite obvious that she didn't like Maddie any more than Maddie liked her.

"Zak's coming back," said Sebastian at last and Maddie looked up, forgetting the princess in the excitement of what was happening.

Zak was indeed coming back, his black wings spread wide as he glided majestically across the sea while below him, leaping and dipping through the waves, were a pair of beautiful blue-grey dolphins.

"Get the boat into the sea," called Zak

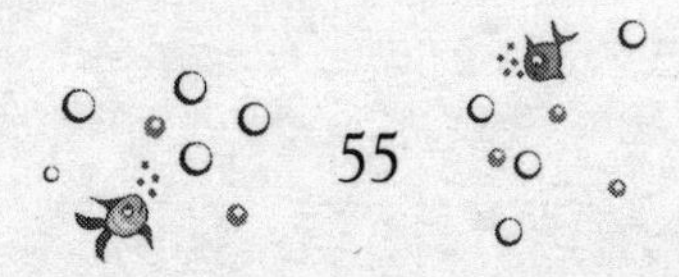

as he landed on the beach. "This is Demetrius," he turned and nodded at the larger of the dolphins, "and his sister, Delphine. They have very kindly offered to tow us across the bay to the Crystal Caves."

Chapter Four

Seraphina

"Hello," said Demetrius. "Are we glad to see you! We were afraid you weren't coming."

"We got here as soon as we could," said Sebastian. "A lot of organization goes into a wish-granting mission."

"Yes, I'm sure," said the dolphin as Sebastian, with Maddie's help, dragged the

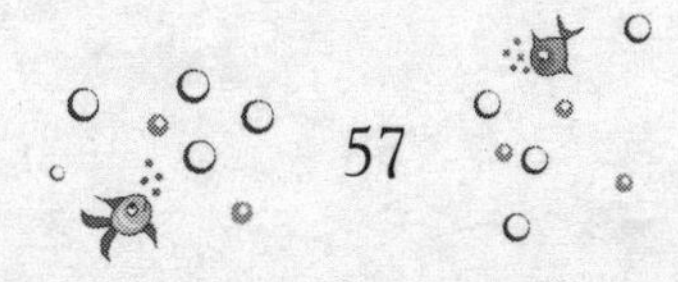

boat to the water's edge. "I only hope you will be able to help."

"The merfolk are in a terrible state," said Delphine the smaller dolphin anxiously, as the friends scrambled aboard the boat.

"Understandable, I suppose, under the circumstances," said Zak. "I guess they are worried about what will happen to Seraphina."

"Yes," Delphine nodded. "They are, of course, but when the comb was stolen, it also brought back memories to them of another theft, a terrible theft that happened many years ago."

"What was stolen that time?" asked Sebastian, as the two dolphins took the tow-rope into their mouths and drew the boat into the gently lapping surf. "Was that a comb as well?"

"No." It was Demetrius who answered,

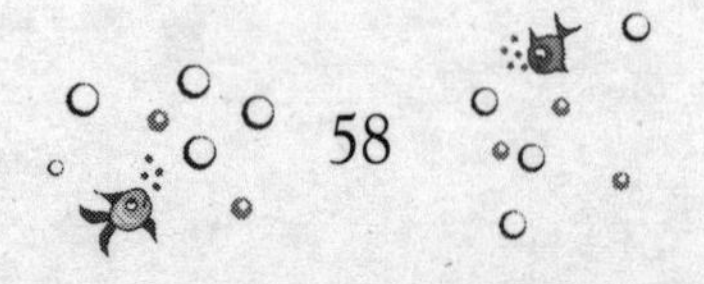

looking over his shoulder. "No, it wasn't a comb that time, it was a merbaby who was stolen."

"A baby?" cried Maddie. "How terrible. Did they get it back?"

"No. Never," said Demetrius grimly. "The baby was never seen again."

"That really is dreadful," said Maddie.

"You may be thinking that a comb is nothing in comparison to a baby," Delphine went on, "but without it, Seraphina will lose her ability to swim and will simply wither away and die."

The friends were silent after that, Maddie and Sebastian sitting side by side amongst the brightly-coloured cushions, while Zak perched behind them, as Delphine and Demetrius drew them swiftly and smoothly across the waves.

The endless blue of the sky soared

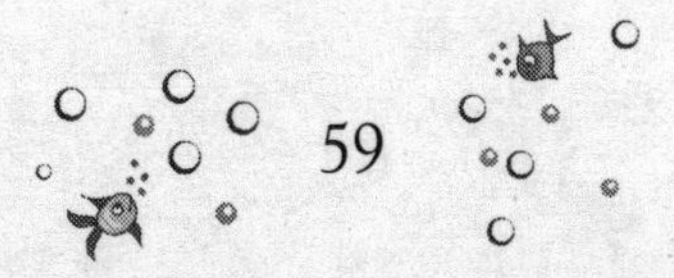

above, while the sunlight glittered on the sea around them and the long, low line of the distant white cliffs grew closer and closer.

"You can see the caves!" cried Sebastian suddenly.

"Oh yes," said Maddie, "and oh, look, look, Sebastian, there are the merfolk! Look, over there on those rocks!"

There were several merfolk sitting on the rocks at the entrance to the caves, their tails in the water. Two of the mermaids were combing their golden hair which tumbled over their shoulders and cascaded over the green fish-like scales of their tails.

As the boat swept by a merman raised his hand in greeting to the friends, who waved back.

"The merfolk are very gentle souls,"

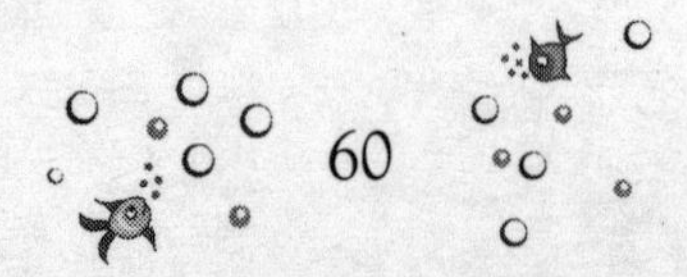

called Demetrius looking back. "They never harm anyone, that is why what is happening to Seraphina is so sad."

Maddie and Sebastian were silent as the dolphins guided the boat between the rocks, and into the cool green darkness of the largest of the caves.

Even Zak was quiet, as if he too was overawed by the majestic splendour of this place. On either side of them tall pillars of pink rock rose from the floor of the cave while from the ceiling, high above, yet more pillars descended almost to the floor. It reminded Maddie of the cathedral she had once visited with her parents.

The water in the centre of the cave was a dark green and looked very, very deep. Maddie wondered what it would be like to fall in and she found herself shivering with fear at the very thought.

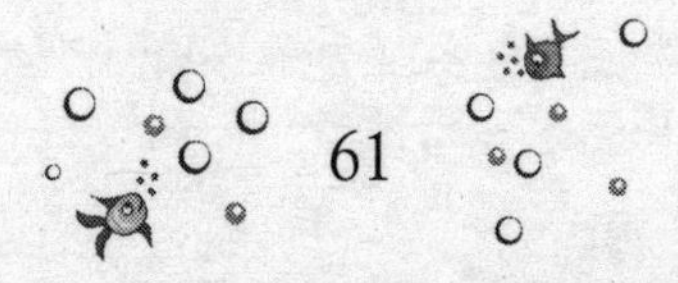

By now the dolphins had drawn the boat into a little backwater and released the tow-rope, after draping it over a rock to secure it.

"This is as far as we can take you," said Delphine. "But here is Silvio. He is Seraphina's nephew and the only person she will see at the moment. He will take you the rest of the way."

The merboy Silvio, who had a mass of beautiful golden curls, gave a shy smile as he beckoned to the friends to follow him. Then with a flash of silver he dived into the water and disappeared.

"I'm not going in there!" muttered Zak.

"We don't have to," said Sebastian. "Look, we can take this path." He pointed to a pathway that ran alongside the water. "Come on," he said, "it's very narrow, but if we keep in single file we shall be all right."

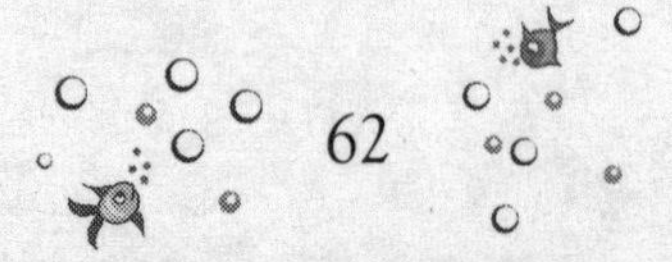

With Zak grumbling and tutting quietly to himself they followed the ripple in the water, which was the only indication that the merboy was still ahead of them as the pathway took them deeper and deeper into the caves.

"How much further do you think it is, Sebastian?" whispered Maddie at last, tugging at his cloak.

"Goodness knows," he murmured, half-turning his head to answer her. "I didn't realize caves could be so deep."

"It's not right," muttered Zak. "I think people forget I'm a bird. Birds aren't supposed to go into the water, neither should they be expected to go underground. Birds were meant to fly, to be as free as the air, to—"

"Shut up, Zak," said Sebastian. "I don't suppose any of us are too keen on this

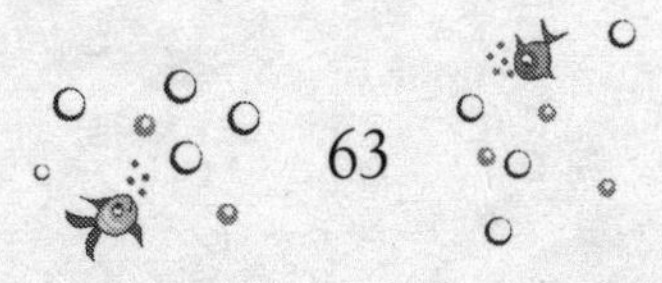

underground bit, but it's no good going on about it. We've agreed to do this and we just have to take whatever comes. . . Oh, I say, look at this!" He stopped suddenly and Maddie bumped into him while Zak careered into the back of her.

"Oh for Pete's sake!" the raven squawked angrily, "Can't you say when you're going to stop? That could have caused a nasty accident, that could. We could have all ended up in the water, and then where would we be, that's what I'd like to know!"

But no one was listening to Zak for before them, quite suddenly, the narrow path alongside the water had opened up into an enormous cavern, with the water flowing into what appeared to be a large pool. Again, as in the smaller caves, pillars of rock soared from the ground and descended from the ceiling, while in one corner a waterfall cascaded down over the rocks, foaming into the deep turquoise of the pool.

Around the cavern, between the pillars, were alcoves and in one of these alcoves, lying on a shelf of rock, Maddie could just make out the dark outline of a figure.

She was about to tell Sebastian when suddenly the merboy, Silvio, surfaced through the water right in front of them, shaking his blond curls and drenching them with thousands of droplets of water.

They all jumped and Zak gave a shriek. "Do you mind!" he squawked indignantly.

"Sorry!" The boy smiled his beautiful, shy smile. "Wait here a moment." With a flick of his tail he moved swiftly across to the alcove where he leaned forward until he was almost out of the water. He appeared to be talking to whoever it was lying on the shelf of rock, then he turned and beckoned the friends forward.

Carefully they picked their way over the wet, slippery rocks around the edge of the water until at last they were standing at the entrance to the dark alcove.

As Maddie's eyes adjusted to the gloom

she saw that the figure lying on the shelf of rock was that of a mermaid, with her tail hanging limply in a small pool of water that had formed between the rocks. But she looked a very different mermaid from those beautiful creatures they had seen lying on the rocks outside. This mermaid had long hair like the others, but theirs

had been golden and silky and hers was a thick, matted, heavy mass that hid her body, while its colour had taken on a dull, metallic, greenish tint.

Even as Maddie stared at her the mermaid lifted her head and stared back with eyes which, although as green as emeralds, were sad, almost lifeless. Then she stretched out one hand in a helpless, pathetic gesture.

"Seraphina?" whispered Maddie uncertainly, taking the hand in hers. The skin felt soft but cold, so cold it was almost clammy.

The mermaid gave a slight nod followed by an even slighter flick of her tail.

"This is Sebastian," said Maddie. "I'm Maddie, and that's Zak."

"We've come to help you," said Sebastian while Zak began nodding his

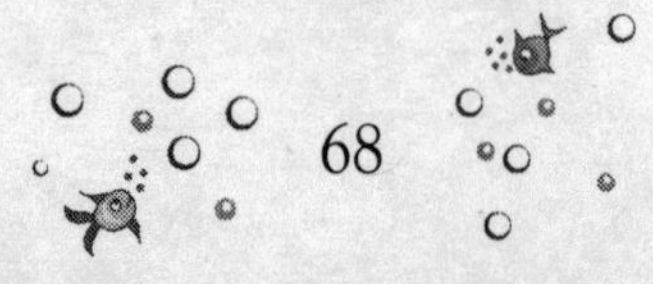

head up and down in agreement.

"I am so ashamed," whispered Seraphina, withdrawing her hand from Maddie's. Her voice was so faint they had to strain their ears to catch what she said. "I don't want anyone to see me looking like this . . . except for Silvio . . . he's such a good boy. He brings me food. . . If it hadn't been for him, I wouldn't still be alive. You see, I can no longer swim. . ."

"We'll help you," cried Maddie. "We'll help you into the water. . . "

"No," said Seraphina, "you don't understand. "Even if you helped me into the water I wouldn't be able to swim because my hair has become so matted and heavy it weighs me down. I need to comb it, you see."

"And that's why we're here," said Sebastian briskly. "We have come to find

whoever stole your comb and to see that it is returned to you."

"That is what the dolphins told me," said Seraphina with a deep sigh. "It is so kind of you to come and to say that you will try to help, but I fear you have had a wasted journey."

"And why's that then?" said Zak, cocking his head on to one side.

"Because I fear that whoever has taken my comb will have taken it to a place where you cannot possibly go."

"Oh, I don't know," said Zak with a shrug. "We seem to get to most places without too much bother."

"Zak, will you please be quiet," said Sebastian.

"OK." In a huff the raven turned his back, but Maddie suspected he was still listening.

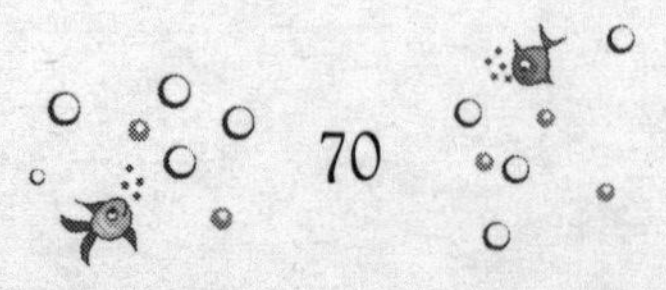

"So why do you think this might be somewhere we can't go?" asked Sebastian, turning back to the mermaid.

"Because if you did, you wouldn't be able to breathe," she said hopelessly. "You see, I fear my comb could well be at the very bottom of the ocean."

"Well, if that's the case, you're absolutely right," said Zak over his shoulder. "There's no way we can go to the bottom of the ocean. I keep telling these guys, I'm a bird for goodness' sake, not a fish!"

"Actually," said Sebastian calmly, ignoring Zak, "there is a way we could go to the bottom of the ocean."

Seraphina lifted her head again and looked at Sebastian in surprise. "How?" she said. "I don't understand."

It was Maddie who answered, Maddie who realized what Sebastian meant.

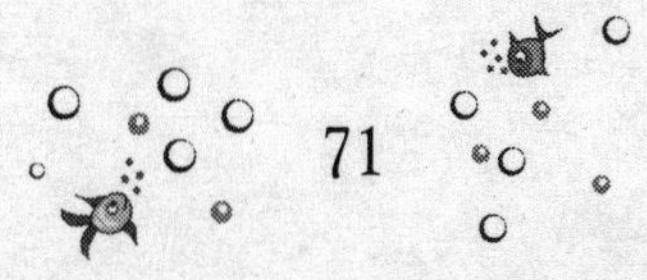

Clasping her hands together she looked up into Seraphina's face. "Sebastian has magic," she whispered.

"Magic?" The mermaid's eyes widened.

"Yes." Maddie nodded, and her curls bobbed frantically. "You see Sebastian is apprentice to Zenith, the WishMaster, and Zenith has given him two magic spells to help him to grant your wish."

Sebastian stepped forward then and spoke. "I had already wondered," he said, "if the first of those spells should be used to enable us to travel underwater. Now if what you say is true, and we may have to go to the bottom of the ocean to look for your comb, I know that I was right."

"Now just you hang on a minute." Zak turned and strutted back to them, a startled look on his face. "I don't like the sound of this at all. I told you before I don't

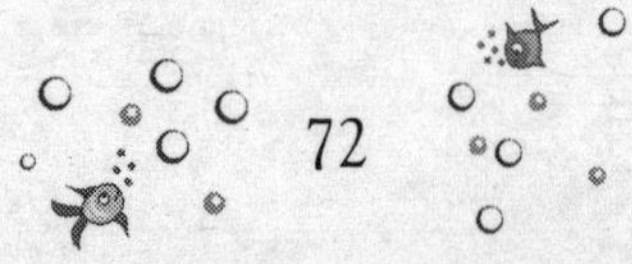

like getting my feathers wet, they go all spiky."

"In that case, Zak, you'd better not come with us," said Sebastian firmly.

"But Zenith said he had to," said Maddie anxiously. "He said he may be of help to us."

"He won't be of any help at all if he keeps on moaning," said Sebastian.

"I can understand him being worried," said Seraphina suddenly.

"Well, I'm glad someone can," said Zak, tossing his head. Then stopping, he peered curiously at the mermaid. "*Why* can you understand?" he said.

"I can understand you being worried about your feathers going spiky if they get wet," she replied. "After all, you are such a handsome bird. . ."

"Oh?" said Zak, cocking his head to one side. "You really think so?"

"Yes," said Seraphina, "I do. And that beautiful blue sheen on your wings must be preserved at all costs."

"Really?" Zak puffed out his chest.

"Yes, so what we would do is have you covered with special oils to protect that magnificent plumage from the salt water," said Seraphina.

"I don't think you need go to all that trouble," said Sebastian, a little impatiently. "If Zak doesn't want to go in the water then he can go up and wait for us with the seagulls."

"It's no trouble," said Seraphina, "but on the other hand, if he really doesn't want to go, I'm sure the seagulls won't mind. . ."

"It's OK," said Zak hastily. "I've changed my mind. I'll go. There's no way I'm staying with those seagulls, I never did like seagulls, they're too full of themselves for

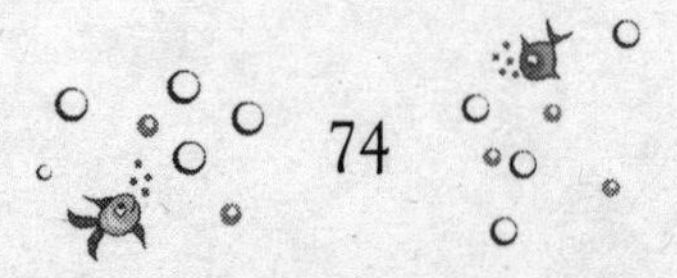

my liking. Besides, I guess it can't be that bad underwater, and if the spell lets us breathe, and Seraphina's oils protect the magnificence of my feathers. . ."

"Right, if that's settled, can we please get on?" said Sebastian impatiently, cutting Zak short.

Seraphina looked out from beneath the mass of her hair at Silvio. "Would you please arrange refreshment and underwater attire for our friends?" she said.

The boy nodded and with another flash of his quick, beautiful smile was gone, into the water and away.

"Doesn't say a lot, does he?" said Zak, cocking his head on one side.

"Maybe you should take a leaf out of his book," said Sebastian.

"Oh, that's charming, that is!" said Zak.

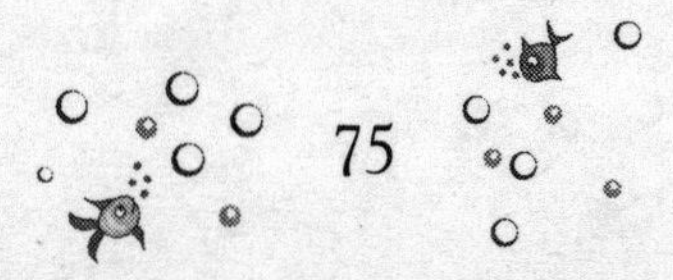

"While we are waiting for Silvio to return," said Sebastian, "perhaps you could tell us about your comb, Seraphina, and how it came to be stolen."

"Cool," said Zak. "I've always wanted to be a detective. Sorry," he said, lapsing into silence again as Sebastian glared at him.

"When did you last have it?" Sebastian went on.

"It has been gone for ten moons now," sighed the mermaid.

"Where did you keep it?" asked Maddie, looking round the cave.

"In my hair," Seraphina replied quietly.

"In your hair!" said Maddie. "You mean. . .?"

"Whoever took it did so whilst I was sleeping," said Seraphina while the friends gaped at her in astonishment.

"How did they get in here?" asked

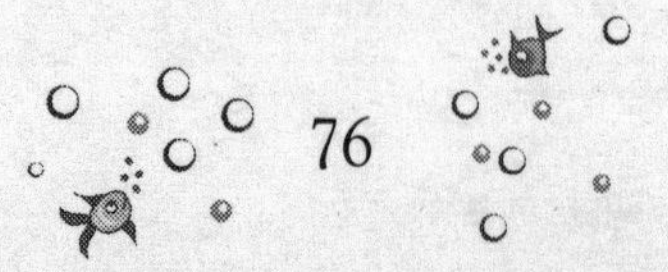

Maddie, looking over her shoulder at the passage they had come through.

"They didn't come that way," said Seraphina, following her gaze, "because Silvio was playing in the pool in the outer cave with the other merchildren, and they would have seen anyone who tried to pass them."

"Then how. . .?" asked Maddie.

Seraphina turned her head and they all moved to see where she was looking.

"The pool?" said Sebastian. "You mean whoever it was came up through the water?"

Seraphina nodded. "Yes," she said, "the pool is very deep and there are many underwater passages through the rocks that lead to the very bed of the ocean."

They were all silent as they considered this. Then Sebastian turned again to the mermaid.

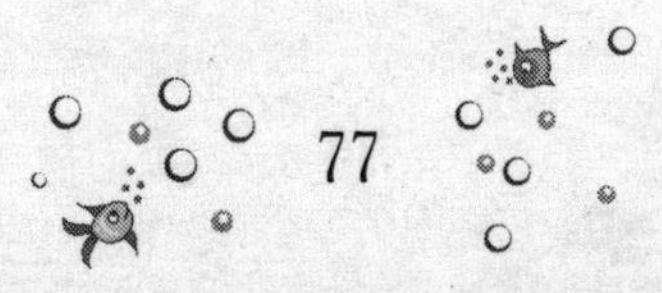

"Right," he said, "so that is the way they came in, and presumably the way they went out again. The next question is, do you have any idea at all who we might be looking for?"

"Not really." Seraphina sighed.

"Zenith the WishMaster said there had been trouble from prawns and other fish – stingrays and barracudas – in this area," said Sebastian thoughtfully. "Could it have been any of those do you think?"

"It is possible," said Seraphina doubtfully.

"The dolphins told us a baby was once stolen from here," said Maddie.

"Yes," said Seraphina, "that is true. It was many years ago now, it happened when I also was a baby. The child's name was Stephano – he was to have been my husband when we grew up. But he was

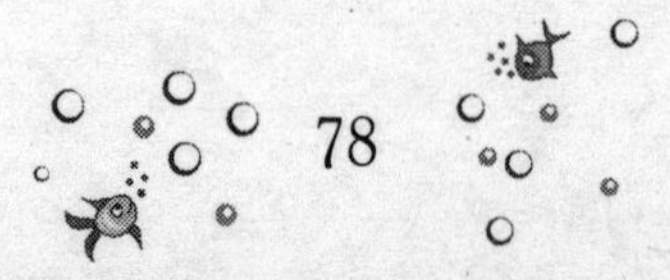

taken away and no one has ever seen him since."

"That's terrible," said Maddie.

"Do you know who stole him?" asked Sebastian.

Seraphina shook her head.

"Could it be the same lot who've stolen your comb?" asked Zak.

"I don't know," said Seraphina helplessly, her eyes filling with tears.

"Did you marry anyone else?" asked Maddie breathlessly, clasping her hands together.

"No," said Seraphina. "We merfolk can only marry the one we are betrothed to when we are born. Since I fear Stephano must be dead, I shall never marry another."

"That is so sad." Maddie gulped and blinked furiously.

"Is there anyone who might know who

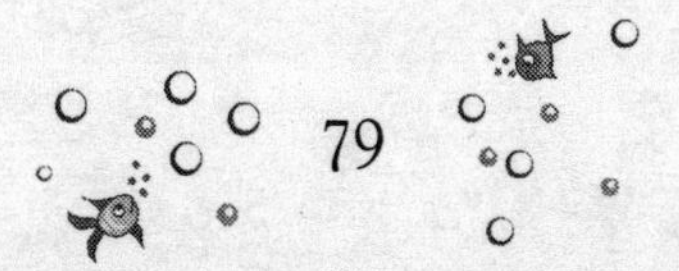

stole your comb?" asked Sebastian, a note of desperation in his voice. "Anyone at all?"

"You could ask Lucius," said Seraphina. "He sees many things and what he doesn't see, he hears about."

"So who is this Lucius?" asked Zak.

"Lucius is a lobster," Seraphina replied.

"Where does he live?" asked Maddie.

"His home is in one of the underwater passages I was telling you about," said Seraphina.

"I think," said Sebastian, "it's high time I performed the spell."

"Oh dear," said Maddie quietly to Zak. "Let's hope he can remember the words. It wouldn't do to get this one wrong."

"You can say that again," sniffed Zak with a worried glance at the deep silent waters of the turquoise pool.

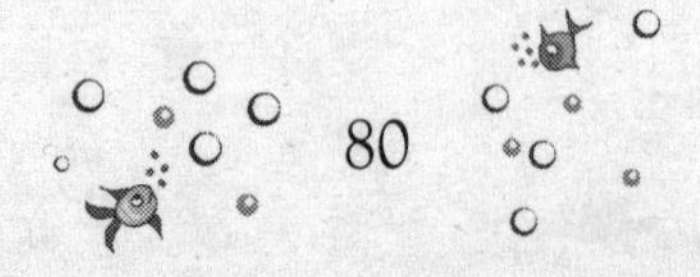

Chapter Five

Into The Deep

"Maybe, Maddie," said Sebastian a little sheepishly, "we could say it together."

"Of course," said Maddie, while Zak gave a snort of laughter. She glared at the raven and he hid his head under his wing.

Together Sebastian and Maddie walked to the edge of the pool and, watched by

Seraphina and Zak, they joined hands and began to chant the first spell.

"Zallaria Zallaria Zalliski,
By the Power of the Mighty Zapphire.
Zaconda Zaconda Zarioka,
Send us the Turquoise Fire!"

As the words echoed around the cavern, and bounced back at them off the towering walls of rock, Sebastian let go of Maddie's hand, took another step forward then lifted his hand high in the air.

As he did so there was a sudden, almost blinding streak of light that caught the aquamarine in the ring he was wearing. The turquoise flash of light illuminated the whole cavern.

"Through this magic," cried Sebastian in a loud voice, "myself, Maddie and Zak

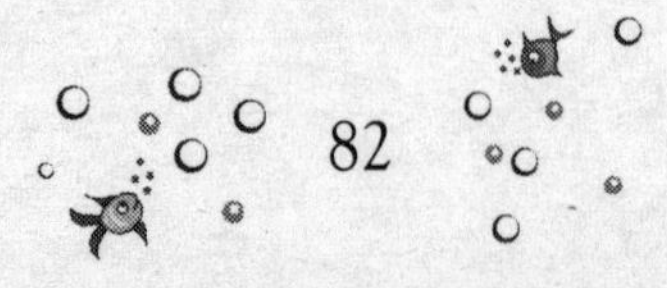

the raven will be given the power to breathe underwater."

There was a second flash, not quite so bright as the first, but still enough to light up the cavern.

Suddenly Maddie was desperate to know whether the magic had worked, but at that moment Silvio returned to the cavern with a platter of mother-of-pearl piled high with exotic fruits.

To her surprise Maddie found she was hungry, and for the moment spells and underwater missions were forgotten as together with the other two she tucked into the delicious fruits.

While they were eating Silvio disappeared once more, only to return a few moments later with yet another salver, this time one containing a pile of neatly folded garments topped by a green bottle with a glass stopper.

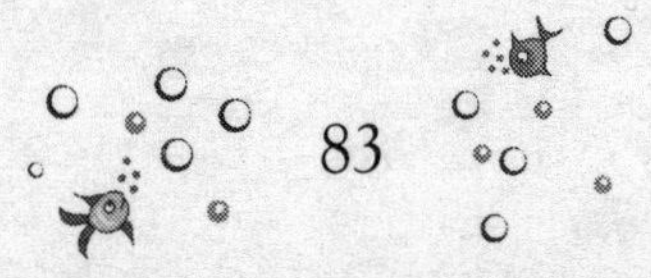

When they had finished eating Seraphina beckoned Maddie into her alcove while Silvio took Sebastian and Zak off to an adjoining one.

"Change into this," said Seraphina, handing Maddie one of the garments. "You will be much more comfortable underwater. Your own clothes would drag you down."

Obediently Maddie changed out of her school uniform and stepped into the garment, which was a sort of cat-suit that covered her legs and arms. It was the same bluey-green sort of colour as Seraphina's tail, made of shiny material that felt both cool and soft against Maddie's skin.

When she was almost ready she caught sight of herself in a long oval mirror at the back of the alcove. For a moment she

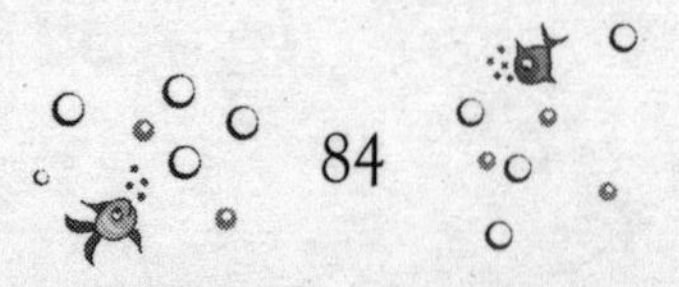

could hardly believe it was herself that stared back at her. She couldn't remember ever liking anything so much before.

At last Maddie stepped out of the alcove and found Sebastian and Zak outside waiting for her. Sebastian's suit was identical to her own but the all-in-one garment made him look taller and more handsome than ever, while Zak with his feathers oiled looked sleek and debonair.

"Hey there!" Zak said when he caught sight of Maddie. "You look like a little sea nymph."

Sebastian smiled and Maddie felt herself blush. Then Sebastian said, "I think we should get started."

"Uh-oh!" squawked Zak. "Here we go. The moment of truth!"

"What do you mean?" said Sebastian indignantly.

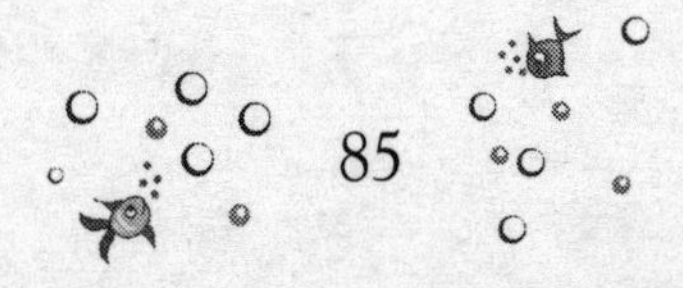

"Let's see whether or not you got the spell right," said Zak, leaning forward and peering into the clear green water.

"Of course it's right," said Sebastian loftily.

"In that case, you won't mind trying it out first, old son, will you?" said Zak. Then leaning forward even more and catching sight of his reflection, he said, "I say, I had quite forgotten just what a handsome fellow you are – the oiled look certainly does something for you. . ."

"Of course I'll go first," said Sebastian, cutting him short. "There's no problem with that." Taking a deep breath he lifted his arms above his head and prepared to dive in.

"Oh, Sebastian," said Maddie urgently, "do be careful, won't you?"

"What do you mean?" Poised on the rim

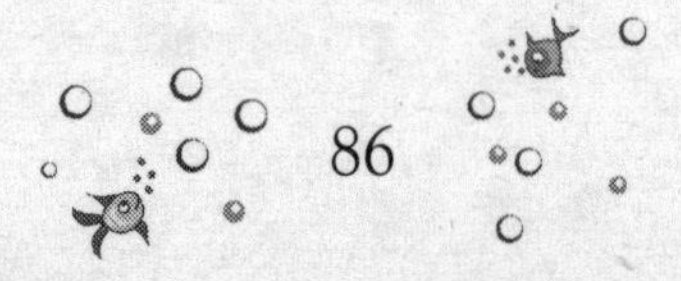

of the pool Sebastian paused and threw her an aloof glance.

"What I mean is if you can't breathe down there you come right back up," she said firmly.

"So you don't believe the spell will have worked either," he said accusingly.

"Oh yes," said Maddie. "I do. Of course I do. But . . . but . . . be careful anyway. . ."

With that he was gone, diving cleanly into the water while the others watched and waited . . . and watched . . . and waited in an agony of suspense.

"Well," said Zak after an unbearable length of time, "he's either having a good look around down there, or he's—"

"Don't!" cried Maddie. "Don't even think that!"

"OK!" Zak shrugged. "I was only—"

But that was as far as he got, for at that

moment Sebastian surfaced in the very middle of the pool. He was laughing, laughing and shaking the water from his eyes.

"It's brilliant!" he cried. "Absolutely wonderful down there! Come on, both of you. It's quite safe. Trust me."

While Maddie and Zak gingerly prepared to dive into the pool Sebastian looked towards Seraphina. "We'll be back," he said. "We will find your comb and we will be back. I promise."

"Silvio will go with you as far as the home of Lucius the lobster," said Seraphina. "Goodbye, goodbye and thank you. . ."

Sebastian was quite right, thought Maddie as she gazed around her in amazement, there was another world under the sea, and it really was quite wonderful.

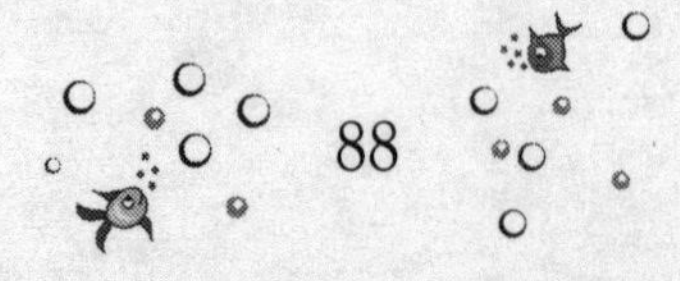

She could see quite clearly through the sparkling green water which was not at all misty or murky as she had feared it might be. It felt strange to be able to breathe but it was not uncomfortable, the only sign that it was in any way unusual being the line of tiny bubbles that rose to the surface from their mouths as they swam.

Maddie was pleased that she had learnt to swim at school. She was able to strike out quite strongly and had no trouble in keeping up with Sebastian. There was, however, a lot of flapping and spluttering from Zak who really looked quite funny as he tackled the crawl with his wings flailing wildly.

All around them were plants of every colour imaginable, some with short spiky leaves, others pink or orange with long trailing fronds that waved and danced

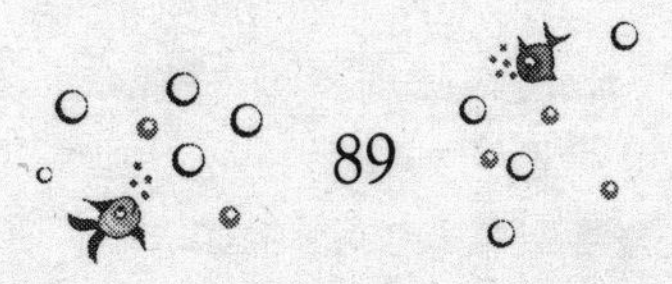

around them as they descended into the deep.

And then there were the fish: fish of all shapes and sizes, big fish and little fish, striped fish and spotted fish, some dark-

coloured, others so transparent you could see right through them. Some swam alone, darting amongst the seaweeds, others were in great shoals that suddenly swept past Maddie and the others, startling them and leaving them gasping at the sheer speed.

And finally there was the seabed itself, soft and sandy with blue and purple rocks and reefs of sharp pink coral. There were shells, bigger and more beautiful than any shells Maddie had ever seen on the beach where she went on holiday; there were starfish, crabs that scuttled away amongst the rocks at their approach, and yet more plants, wide brown ribbon-like strands, pink feathery tendrils and green slippery leaves.

Silvio swam ahead of them, peering from left to right, his golden curls like a

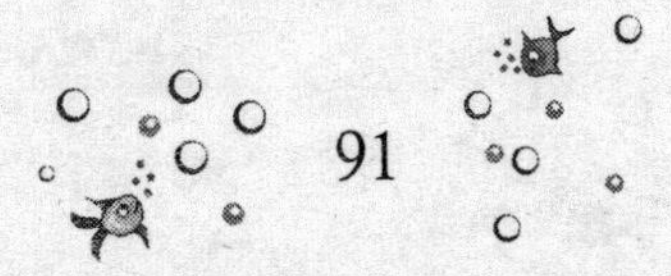

halo around his head. For once even Zak was silent as if he too was overwhelmed by his surroundings.

At last Silvio stopped, then beckoning to the others to follow him he darted away between pillars of pinkish-grey rock.

"Come on, Maddie." His voice sounding strange and echoey, Sebastian took her hand and with Zak close behind them, they followed the merboy between the opening in the rocks.

The water was not quite so clear here in this part, Maddie thought, as she peered through the gloom. Fish appeared suddenly, hugely magnified, looming up, staring at them with unblinking eyes, then with a flick of their tails turning and darting away.

And then, at last, Silvio stopped again, this time before what looked like a large

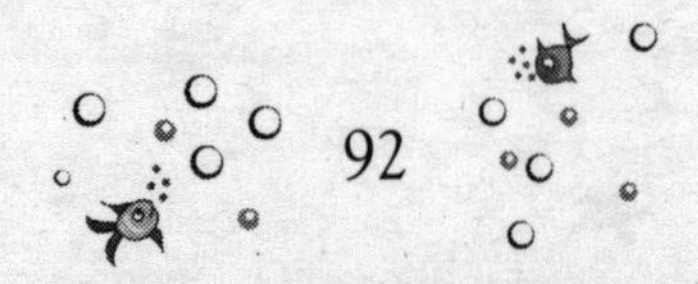

cage wedged between two pieces of coral.

"Lucius?" he called. "Are you there?"

"It's an old lobster pot," said Maddie, and her voice sounded strange even to herself, strange in a bubbly sort of way.

Even as they watched, a huge, greenish-coloured lobster with quite wicked-looking claws looked out at them between the bars.

"Yes?" he said abruptly. "What do you want? Is that you, Silvio?" He peered at the merboy. "What are you doing down here?"

"I've brought these people to see you," said Silvio. "This is Sebastian, he is apprentice to Zenith, the WishMaster. And this is Maddie, his friend."

"Ahem!" coughed Zak.

"Oh sorry," said Silvio. "And this is Zak, the raven."

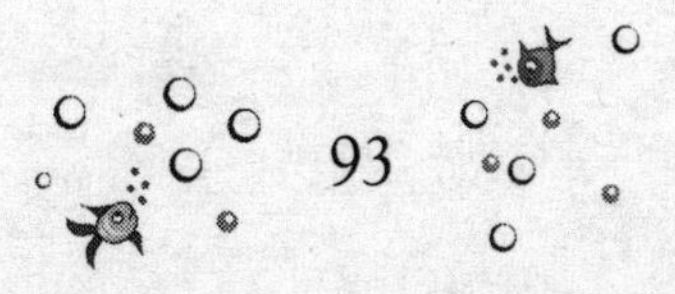

"He doesn't look like a raven," said the lobster suspiciously.

Maddie turned and looked at Zak. It was true, he didn't look like a raven at that precise moment with his wet feathers slicked back from his sharp beak – he looked more like a very thin cormorant and Maddie was forced to stifle a giggle.

"Well, what do you expect!" snapped Zak. "I keep telling everyone I'm a bird and that birds aren't supposed to go underwater – but will they listen? Anyway," he eyed the lobster up and down, "I wonder how you would fare if you suddenly found yourself up in the sky!"

"No fear of that," said the lobster. "I can't stand heights, so I wouldn't be so stupid as to—"

"I'll have you know," interrupted Zak, "I

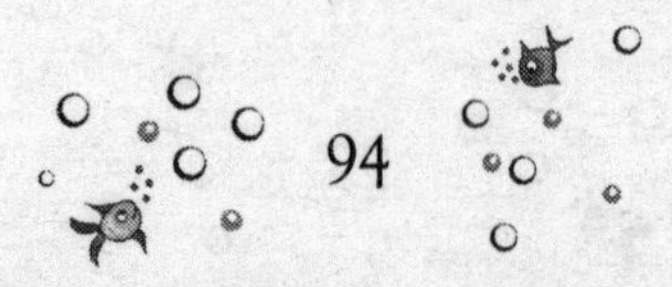

didn't have a lot of choice. I—"

But Silvio intervened, cutting him short. "These people are hoping you may be able to help them," he said.

"Wait a minute," said the lobster. "I'll come out."

"Can he get out ?" whispered Maddie. "I thought lobsters got trapped in those pots."

"Not this one," murmured Silvio. "He got his friend the swordfish to cut the rope, then he persuaded him to cut a door in the side of the pot and that's where he's lived ever since."

Sure enough, even as Silvio was speaking, a door in one side of the pot swung back and the lobster slipped out.

"That's better," he said. "Now, what is it you want?"

"It's all to do with Seraphina," said Silvio.

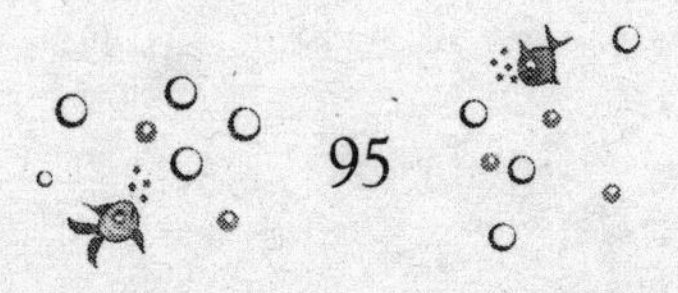

"Eh? Seraphina?" the lobster looked startled. "Why, what's wrong with her?"

"Her comb has been stolen," said the merboy.

"Oh, my giddy aunt!" The lobster blinked and waved his claws in the air. "That *is* serious. What's she going to do about it?"

"That's why we are here," explained Sebastian. "You see, Seraphina made a wish that her comb be returned to her, and Zenith the WishMaster has sent us to grant her wish."

"Zenith, you say?" mused the lobster thoughtfully. "I've heard of him. His magic is famous, even down here. So what is it you think I can do to help?"

"The comb was stolen ten moons ago," said Silvio. "We wondered if you saw anything about that time that might help."

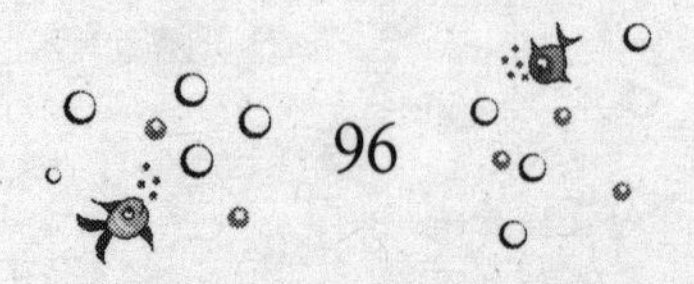

"Ten moons ago, you say?" said the lobster. "Now, let me think. No," he said, at last, shaking his head. "I don't think so. . . Oh, wait a minute, there was something about that time, now I come to think of it."

"Oh," said Maddie. "What was that?"

"Barracudas," said the lobster.

"Barracudas?" whispered Silvio, and there was no mistaking the terror in his eyes.

"Yes." The lobster glanced over his shoulder, then lowered his voice. "Very late at night," he went on, "a whole shoal of them, moving as if the very devil was after them. They swept through here like a dose of salts and I wondered at the time what they'd been up to. It did go through my mind, I have to admit, that they must have been up to no good at that time of night."

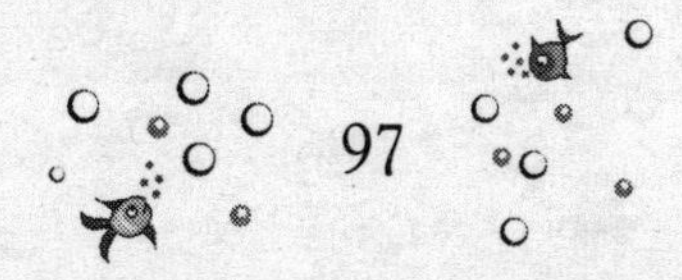

"So do you think they could have stolen Seraphina's comb?" said Maddie.

The lobster peered at her "I suppose there's always the chance it was them. And," he added darkly, "I wouldn't put anything past them."

"But why would they want her comb?" asked Sebastian with a frown. "Have barracudas got hair?"

"Of course not," Lucius replied scornfully. "They probably just wanted it for their own treasure trove. The barracudas must be worth a fortune these days. They've amassed a vast horde of valuables. On the other hand, maybe they are going to sell it. Mermaids' combs would fetch a very good price on the murky market."

"I can't see why," said Maddie. "They are only of any use to the mermaid herself, after all."

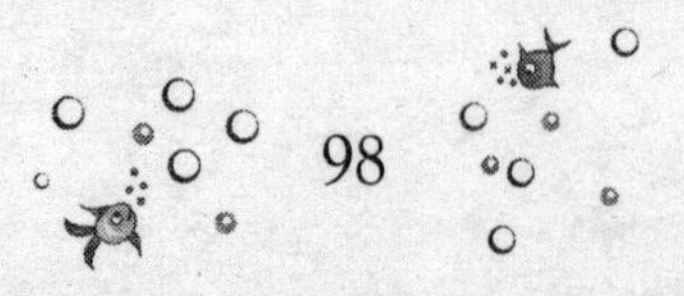

"Collectors would buy them," said the lobster. "And the barracudas know that."

"So where would we find these barracudas?" asked Zak. "Where do they hang out?"

"They live in the Rainbow Lagoon," Lucius replied.

"Could you take us there?" asked Sebastian.

"No fear." Lucius shook his head. Then with a slight whine in his voice he went on, "I don't leave my pot much these days. Rheumatism in my claws, you see. But I'll tell you what I will do. I'll point you in the right direction. You'll have to take care though. Power-crazy those barracudas are, and vicious with it."

"I'm afraid I can't go any further with you either," said Silvio. "I have to return

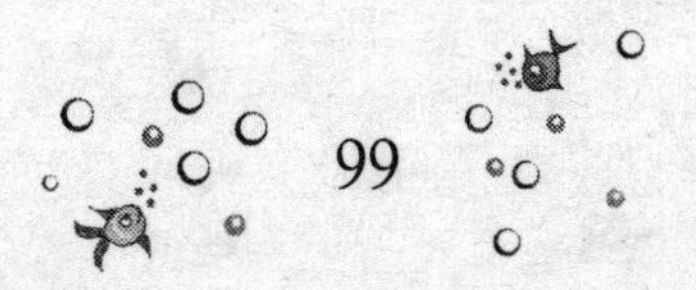

to Seraphina. But Lucius will give you all the directions you need."

"Oh dear," said Maddie. "This looks very much as if we are going to be on our own from now on."

"So what's new!" said Zak, hunching his shoulders. "Story of our lives."

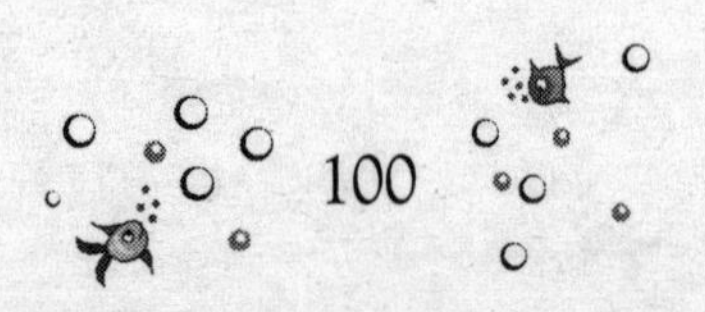

Chapter Six

Pieces of Eight

After taking their leave of Lucius the lobster and waving farewell to Silvio, the friends swam on through all the glories of the underwater world in their search for the Rainbow Lagoon, home of the deadly barracudas.

Maddie was just beginning to feel tired and was wondering how much further

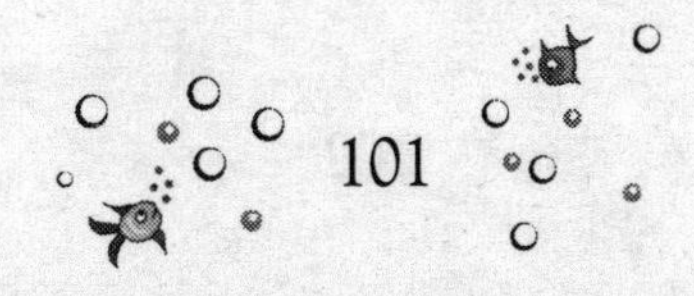

they had to go when Zak, who was a little way ahead, suddenly stopped, listened, then did a rapid U-turn and streaked back to them.

"What is it?" asked Sebastian urgently.

"Blessed if I know," said Zak. "Some sort of kerfuffle up ahead. The most almighty din, and whatever it is seems to be coming this way. I think we'd better take cover – come on, over there behind that reef."

Together they darted behind the coral reef and crouched down on the seabed as the sound of the commotion drew closer.

"It sounds like some sort of battle," whispered Maddie.

"I think you could be right," Sebastian agreed. Then clutching her arm he said, "Yes, you are right. Just look at that!"

A great tangle of fish had come into view engaged in the fiercest of battles.

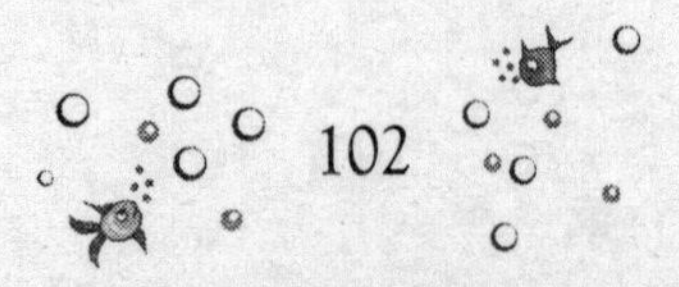

Some of the fish had flattish, triangular-shaped bodies with whip-like tails that cracked and hissed as they attacked.

"Stingrays," whispered Maddie. "I've seen pictures of them in my encyclopaedia at home."

"What are those other fish?" Sebastian whispered back. "They are bigger, and just as vicious."

"I don't know," said Maddie. "They look really wicked. Just look at their teeth, they're so sharp."

Even as they watched, two of the fish, locked in the fiercest of combat, whipped towards the friends' hiding place while at the same time the water around them clouded red with blood.

"Oh my hat!" gasped Zak, putting both wings over his head. "Time for another spell, old son, wouldn't you say?"

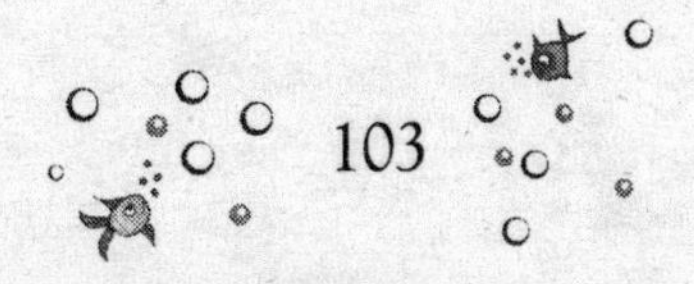

"Keep down!" snapped Sebastian. "We can't use the other spell yet."

"So how do you propose we get out of this?" said Zak, peering through the coral at the battle which raged all around them. "Just walk through them and hope they don't notice us?"

"We wait," said Sebastian firmly, ignoring Zak's sarcasm. "They haven't seen us, and they certainly haven't heard us with all that racket they are making, so there's a good chance they'll never know we are here."

The battle continued and the friends watched from their hiding-place as first the stingrays seemed to be gaining the upper hand and then the other, larger fish.

"They're going," said Sebastian in relief at last as the bigger fish surged past the

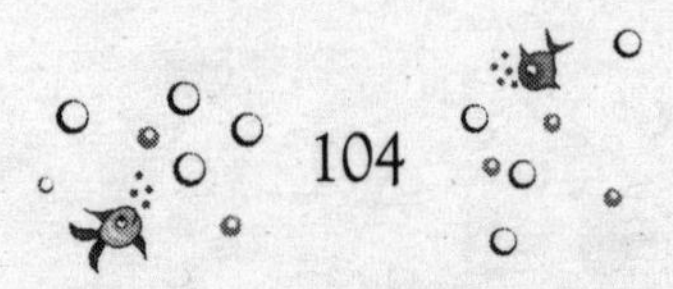

coral reef in pursuit of the remaining stingrays. "Come on, let's go before they come back."

"Do you think it's safe?" asked Maddie, her eyes wide with fear.

Cautiously Sebastian peered over the top of the coral reef. "Yes," he said at last, "Come on, they've gone."

They crept out of their hiding-place and swam on but everything was silent now and very, very still.

"All the other fish and sea creatures must still be in hiding," said Maddie, fearfully peering from left to right as she swam.

"You can't blame them," said Zak. "No one would want to get caught up in a battle like that."

"I'm glad we didn't have to use the other spell," said Sebastian with a

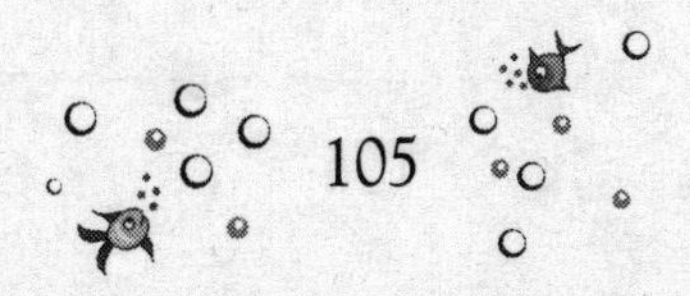

shudder. "We may well need it to help us *after* we've found the comb, not before."

Together they struck out again and swam on through the still, silent waters.

And then, gradually, the water became misty, so misty that it appeared almost milky in places. They were entering another rocky area and this time weeds as thick as vines trailed in great loops from the tops of the columns of rock right down to the very seabed.

"I don't like it," whispered Maddie. "It's scary."

It was still very quiet with barely any movement when, quite suddenly, through the misty waters, a large shape loomed up before them and they all jumped.

"Jeepers!" squawked Zak. "What in the world is that?"

"It's a ship," breathed Sebastian. "Or

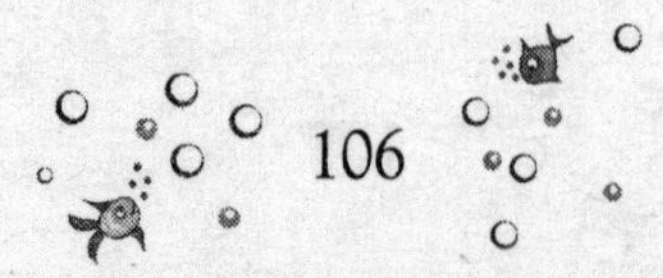

rather, I should say it was once a ship. It's now a wreck."

"Oh yes!" said Maddie, clutching hold of Sebastian's hand while Zak perched nervously on her shoulder. "It looks like one of those galleons that they had in the olden days. I've been learning about them at school. They used to carry priceless treasures and they would be attacked by pirates."

"Pirates?" muttered Zak dubiously. "Didn't they used to capture parrots?"

"Yes." Sebastian looked at him and laughed. "And they made them sit on their shoulders. You'd be good at that, Zak."

With an indignant croak Zak moved smartly from Maddie's shoulder.

"I think it looks spooky," said Maddie slowly, screwing up her eyes.

"Maybe it's haunted," muttered Zak uneasily.

"Oh dear," said Maddie uncomfortably, eyeing the ship. "Do you really think so? Who do you think might haunt it? The captain, or one of the sailors, perhaps? Or even a pirate who maybe got trapped on the ship before it went down."

"Do be quiet Maddie," squawked Zak. "You are making my feathers stand on end. There probably isn't anything on there at all."

"Well, there's only one way to find out, and we won't know if we just stand here looking at it," said Sebastian. "Come on, follow me. Keep close together and be quiet. We don't want to go disturbing any ghosts."

The galleon was tilted crazily to one side, its tall masts broken, but still with

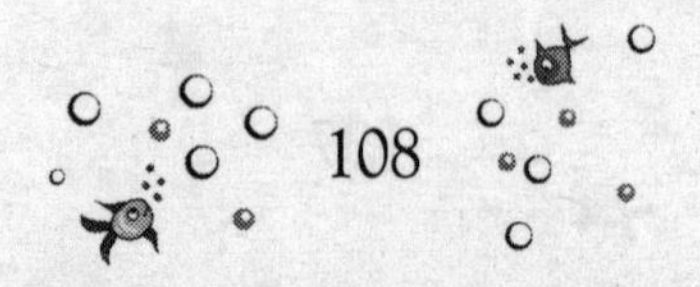

tattered scraps trailing from the sails. Its huge rotting hulk was covered in barnacles and green with algae, but traces of its name in ornate gilt lettering could just be seen on the bows.

"The *Golden Fleece*," whispered Maddie in awe.

"She must have been beautiful in her day," Sebastian whispered back. "Come on, we'll swim to the top and then we can get on to the deck."

The deck of the once proud and stately galleon had almost rotted away and there were gaping holes in the planks. Small fish spilled out of the hold, obviously startled by the friends' approach, and darted away through the milky water to hide in dark portals or in rotting cavities in the wood.

"We can get in down there," whispered Sebastian, staring down into the hold.

"Oh boy!" wailed Zak softly. "Do you think we should?"

"Yes," said Sebastian, "something is telling me that we may find a clue to the missing comb here."

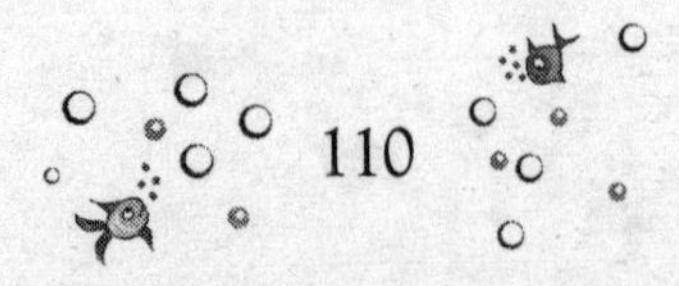

"I'm scared," whispered Maddie.

"Don't be," said Sebastian. "I'll look after you."

"I've heard that one before," said Zak. "What I'd like to know is who looks after you? Me, I suppose!"

But Sebastian wasn't listening. Instead he was leading the way into the ship's hold.

It was dark, quiet, full of shadows and strange shapes. They were probably only pieces of the ship's furniture but now, decayed and rotting, they loomed ominously above with strands of seaweed twisting and curling around them like hair.

The friends swam forward peering cautiously from left to right.

Suddenly, with an excited squawk, Zak began flapping his wings. The other two,

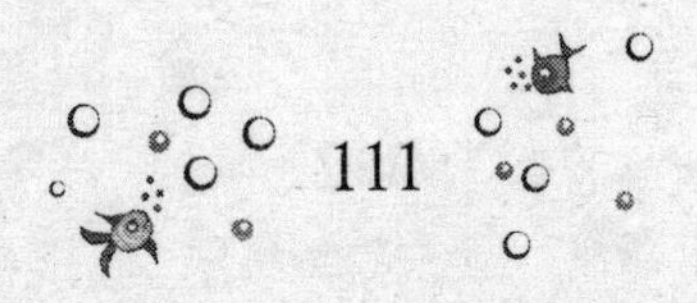

who had gone on ahead, turned and swam back to him.

"What is it, Zak?" asked Sebastian.

"Over there." Zak was nodding his head, up and down, as if in his excitement he couldn't stop. "Look! Pieces of eight! Pieces of eight!"

Maddie turned, then gasped at what she saw. In one corner of the hold was a rusty chest, its lid thrown back to reveal a horde of gold coins and precious jewels: necklaces, bracelets and rings.

"Oh!" she cried, as with her eyes as wide as saucers she moved forward towards the chest, but even as she reached out to touch the treasure, there was a sudden movement from the shadows in one of the dark corners of the hold. They barely had time even to turn and see what it was before a snake-like tentacle whipped out across the floor and wrapped itself around Maddie's ankle, grasping it in a vice-like grip.

She let out a shriek. "Oh Sebastian!" she cried. "What is it? It's got my foot!"

Before Sebastian could even move, a second tentacle shot out, then a third, waving around, trying to ensnare other limbs.

It was Zak who came to the rescue. Zak who streaked forward, pecking mercilessly with his sharp beak at the tentacle that held Maddie.

A blood-curdling shriek of rage filled the air, then as Maddie felt her foot released, the water around them suddenly darkened, clouded with a dense, billowing, blue-black liquid.

Maddie screamed as they were plunged into darkness. "Sebastian! Sebastian!" she cried. "Where are you?"

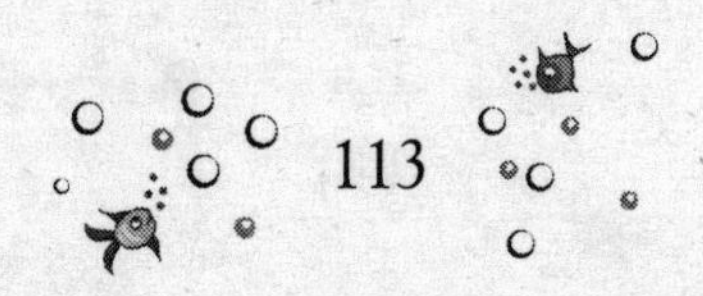

But there was only silence, a terrifying silence that led Maddie to believe she was alone.

She felt panic rise in her throat, blind panic, then as she thrashed about in the dark clouded water she felt someone grasp her hand. For one horrifying moment she thought it was one of those tentacles again but the next instant fingers closed around her own, and to her utmost relief, she knew it was Sebastian's hand that held hers.

"Sebastian. . .!" Her voice was choked, bubbly in its terror.

"It's all right," he said and his voice was reassuringly close.

"We have to get out," she gasped.

"Yes. . ." Sebastian replied. "The spell. . . Come on Maddie, we'll say it together. . . Now!"

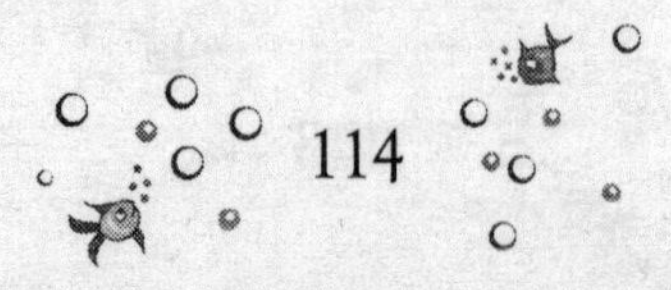

"Zambazine of Zizabar—"

"No!"

The command came from Zak and Sebastian and Maddie both froze in the darkness. "Don't use the spell!"

"But. . ."

"Just go! Now! Get to the surface! I'm right behind you! Go! Go! Go!"

Together they swam through the rapidly darkening waters and out of the hold, then striking out they swam away from the wrecked *Golden Fleece* and up and up, until at last, gasping and spluttering, they surfaced, breaking through the waves.

"That was terrifying," choked Maddie, still clutching at Sebastian. "What do you think that awful thing was?"

"Goodness knows," gasped Sebastian shaking water from his eyes. "But whatever it was, it certainly wasn't a ghost."

When Maddie had recovered a little she looked curiously around her. They were in a quiet bay with water of the deepest green, while around the edges, beyond the white sand of the beach, palm trees waved in the soft breeze.

"Come on," said Sebastian. "Let's swim for the shore, we can rest there."

"All right," said Maddie. Then glancing around her she said anxiously, "Where's Zak?"

"He'll be around," Sebastian replied. "Don't worry."

Together they struck out for the shore and moments later they trailed wearily out of the waves and flung themselves down on to the white sands beneath the waving palms.

It was Maddie who noticed it first. High above them in the bright blue of the sky

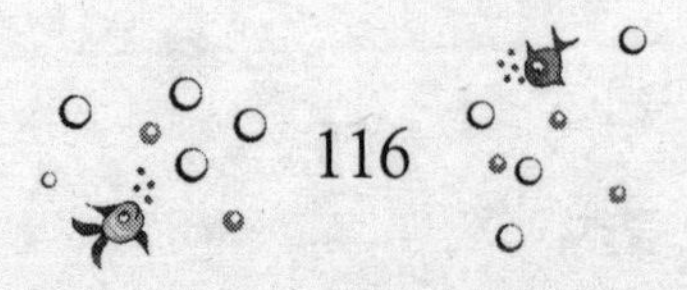

not one, but two arcs of colour spanned the pool.

"Look!" she breathed. "There are two rainbows, Sebastian. This must be it. The Rainbow Lagoon."

"If that's the case, it's also the home of the deadly barracudas," said Sebastian slowly.

"Do you think that's what that creature that attacked us was – a barracuda?" whispered Maddie.

"I don't know," said Sebastian. "Honestly, Maddie, I really don't know." He was lying on his back in the sand as he spoke, his eyes closed, his arms flung wide.

"All the jewellery in that chest could have been their treasure trove!" Maddie went on excitedly. "Oh Sebastian, Seraphina's comb could have been in there."

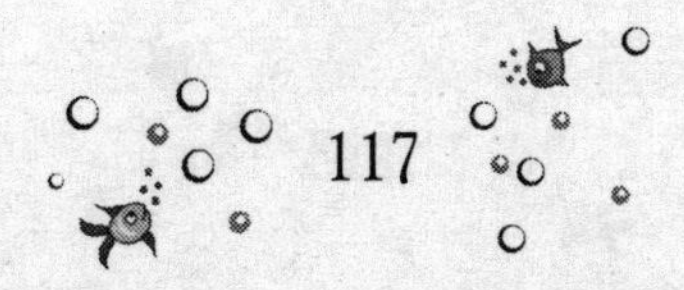

She paused, then gazing anxiously across the lagoon she said, "There's no sign of Zak yet. He hasn't surfaced. He's still down there, Sebastian. Oh, what do you think has happened to him?"

"He said he was right behind us. . . He's usually more than capable of taking care of himself." Sebastian spoke calmly, but he sat up, shielding his eyes from the bright sunshine, and stared across the lagoon.

"I know that," said Maddie uneasily. "But that thing, whatever it was, supposing it got him with one of those wicked tentacles. It got me, Sebastian, and it was Zak who rescued me. He pecked at it until it let me go. Sebastian, we have to do something. We can't just leave him down there. It might have got hold of him. It might squeeze him to death! Sebastian, I can't bear it! We've got to do something."

By this time even Sebastian was getting concerned. He scrambled to his feet and anxiously began scanning the waves.

At last he turned to Maddie. "I'll have to go down there again," he said.

"I'll come with you," she said bravely. It was the last thing she wanted to do – to go back down there through those murky waves to that ghostly old galleon with the creature, whatever it was, that lurked inside. But on the other hand, she couldn't bear to think of Zak in deadly danger.

"No," said Sebastian sharply. "You stay here."

"But what will you do?"

"If it comes to it, I shall use the second spell."

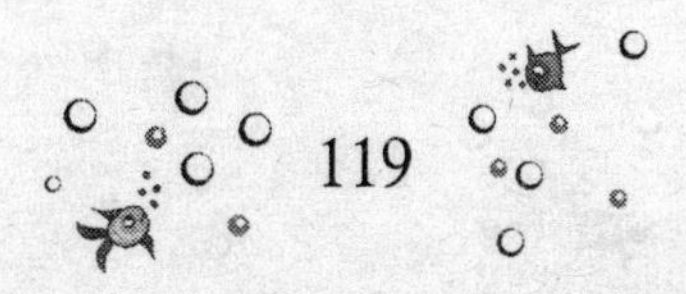

"In that case, I shall definitely come with you," said Maddie firmly. "Because if I don't, there's a very good chance you might forget the words, then it'll go wrong."

Sebastian hesitated, then he said, "All right, we'll go together."

Taking Maddie's hand he helped her to her feet, and together they ran back to the water's edge.

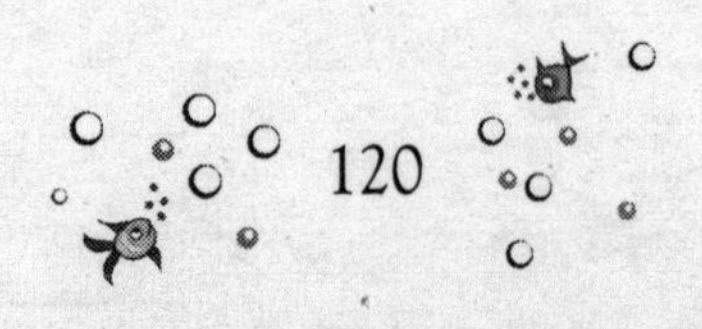

Chapter Seven

The Octopus

It was still murky beneath the waves, with that strange bluish-black substance clouding the water.

"What do you think it is?" whispered Maddie, holding tightly to Sebastian's hand as they swam closer and closer to the wreck of the *Golden Fleece*.

"I don't know," Sebastian admitted.

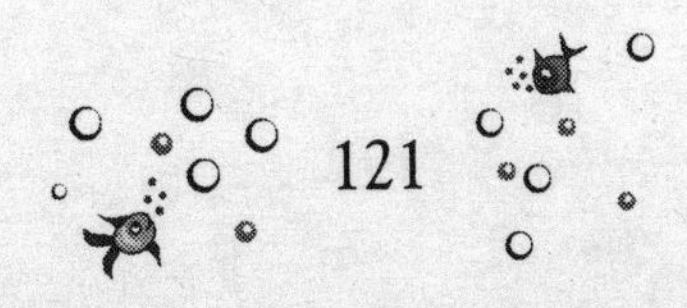

"But whatever it is, it certainly slows you down. It's a bit like a thick fog, except that it's coloured."

"I wonder where Zak is," said Maddie fearfully, as the ghostly shape of the galleon suddenly loomed up before them once again.

"I dread to think," said Sebastian, then he stopped and lifted his head.

"What's the matter?" hissed Maddie.

"Listen. That noise. What is it?" said Sebastian with a frown.

"I can't hear anything," said Maddie. Then, "Oh, wait a minute, yes I can . . . it sounds like Zak," she breathed. "Yes. It is Zak! Oh, Sebastian, he's squawking! What do you think that awful thing is doing to him?"

"I don't know," said Sebastian grimly. "But I mean to find out. If it's hurt

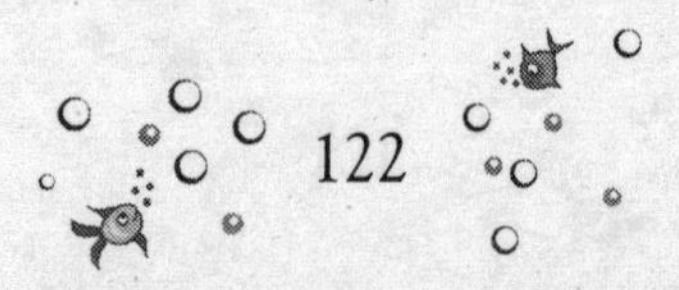

Zak then it has me to answer to!"

Keeping very close together they cautiously approached the wreck once more. At last, silently, they were able to slip over the side on to the deck again.

"He's still making that noise," whispered Maddie. "Perhaps that creature is holding Zak prisoner. . ."

"Wait a minute," said Sebastian suddenly and they both paused to listen again. "He's not squawking," he said incredulously after a moment. "He's laughing, for goodness' sake!"

Indignantly, with Maddie right behind him, he burst through the entrance of the hold into the room where they had first seen the treasure, and there, perched on a tall post of rotting wood, was Zak. He certainly didn't look as if he was in trouble, neither did he look as if anyone was holding him against his will.

Maddie's gaze flew to the chest and there, draped over the treasure, was the strangest looking creature she had ever seen. It was huge, with a fat, black body, eight very long tentacles that waved about in the water and a pair of very round, beady, black eyes.

"Zak, what do you think you're doing?" demanded Sebastian, quite crossly, but at the same time keeping a wary eye on the creature.

"Oh, hi there, you guys!" Zak cocked his head on to one side and eyed them up and down. "What have you come back for?"

"Well, what do you think we've come back for!" Sebastian almost exploded.

"We were worried about you, Zak," said

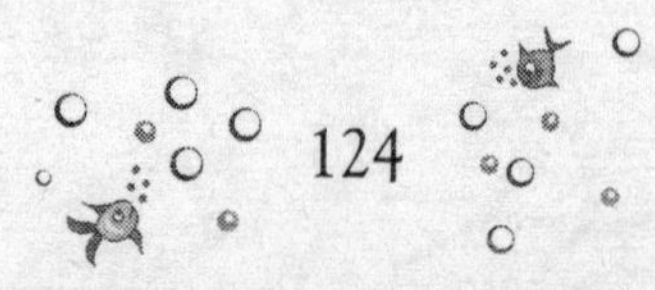

Maddie. "We thought something had happened to you. We came back to rescue you."

"Is that a fact?" Zak looked pleased and puffed out his chest.

"Sebastian was even going to use the second spell to help you if you were in trouble," said Maddie.

"I didn't know you cared that much, old son!" said Zak with a cackle.

"I won't another time, I can tell you," snapped Sebastian crossly. "Why didn't you follow us? What do you think you're playing at, you silly creature!"

"Oi, we'll have less of that talk if you don't mind," squawked Zak.

"Well, just in case you've forgotten, we are on a mission and you are wasting time," said Sebastian crossly. Turning his head he threw another curious glance at the strange-looking creature on the treasure chest.

"Oh, wasting time am I? Is that what you call it?" said Zak sarcastically. "Well, clever-clogs, I'll have you know I've made more progress in the last half hour than the two of you put together. . ."

"What do you mean?" asked Maddie. She also was keeping an eye on the strange-looking creature and staying well out of its way, mindful of how it had trapped her foot before.

"This," said Zak, nodding at the creature, "is Oscar."

"Is he a barracuda?" asked Sebastian.

Zak gave a squawk of laughter. "Whatever makes you think that?"

"Well, while you've been down here gossiping, we have found out that this actually happens to be the Rainbow

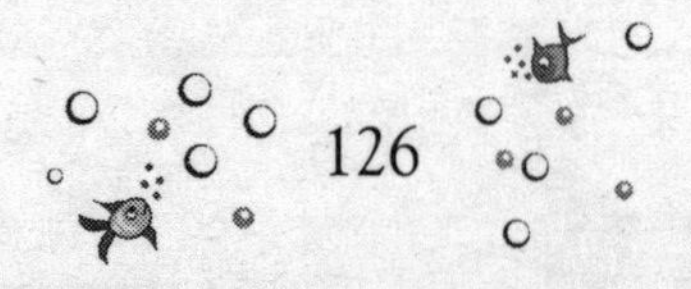

Lagoon," said Sebastian, rather huffily Maddie thought, as if he was still very annoyed with Zak. "And," he went on stiffly, "according to Lucius, the Rainbow Lagoon is home to the barracudas."

"That's absolutely right," Zak agreed. "Not only do the barracudas live in the Rainbow Lagoon, their actual home is right here in the *Golden Fleece*. Isn't that right, Oscar?"

"Certainly is." The creature spoke so unexpectedly it made Maddie jump.

"So if he isn't a barracuda, what exactly is he?" said Sebastian eyeing the creature up and down.

"Oscar," said Zak importantly, "is an octopus."

"I don't care," said Maddie indignantly, "because whatever he is it certainly

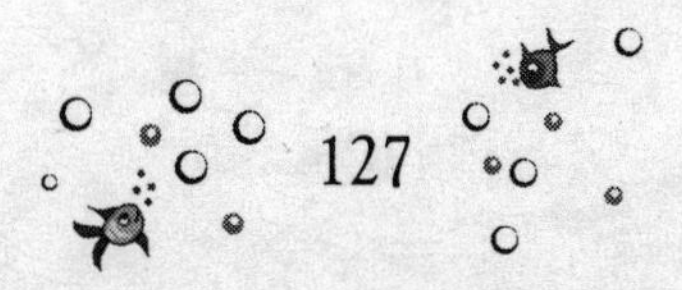

doesn't give him the right to frighten people the way he frightened us."

"He was only doing his job," said Zak stoutly, defending his new friend. "Actually, he's a first-rate fellow, aren't you, Oscar?"

"Certainly am," said the octopus.

"And what, pray, is his job, exactly?" asked Sebastian haughtily.

"He's head of security down here," said Zak. "He's a very good security guard as well. He tackled me, I can tell you, but when he felt the full force of my beak he was so impressed he wanted to know what line of business I was in. I told him, we actually have quite a bit in common."

"What are you talking about?" Sebastian stared at Zak in astonishment.

"I told him," said Zak, "I also am in charge of security. . ."

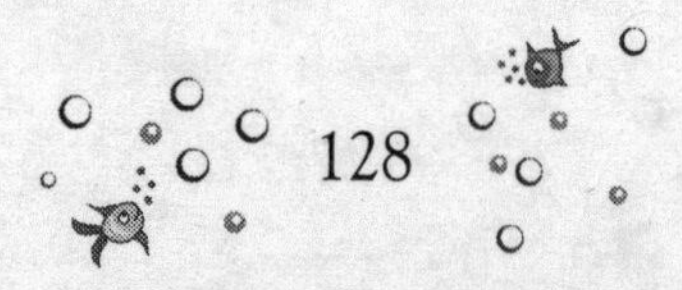

"What?" spluttered Sebastian.

"For Zenith the WishMaster no less, at the East Tower in Zavania's Royal Palace. He was even more impressed with that!"

"Huh!" said Sebastian with a snort, then as Maddie gently touched his arm he appeared to calm down. "So who does he work for?" he said turning to stare at the octopus.

"The barracudas," said Zak. "Or rather, he used to work for them, he's handed in his notice. Haven't you, Oscar old chap?"

"Certainly have," said Oscar.

"Oh?" said Maddie curiously. "Why is that?"

"He says they are mean, they don't pay enough, and he says he's fed up with the way they keep on waging war on everyone else. That was them we saw fighting with the stingrays you know."

"Oh dear," said Maddie glancing fearfully over her shoulder. "I hope they don't come back yet." Then turning, but still warily, to the creature, she said, "Maybe you can tell us Mr Oscar, was it the barracudas who stole Seraphina's comb?"

"Certainly was," said the octopus.

"So what did they do with it?" asked Sebastian, eyeing the treasure that was just visible underneath the body and tentacles of the strange-looking creature. "Is it in there with the rest of the treasure?"

"Apparently not." It was Zak who answered the question from his perch on the top of the rotting post. "Oh, normally it would have been put in with the rest of the treasure trove, but Oscar tells me this particular item is a bit different. Isn't that so, Oscar?"

"Certainly is," said the octopus.

"This time," Zak went on, "the barracudas didn't keep the comb for themselves. It seems they have sold it to someone else."

"Do we know who?" asked Sebastian, looking from Zak to the octopus then back to Zak again.

"Not exactly," said Zak. "What Oscar does know though is where the barracudas took the comb after they had stolen it."

"Oh?" said Sebastian. "And where is that?"

"To a city called Tritonia," said Zak importantly. "A city which was once home to a great civilization."

"So where is it then, this city?" asked Sebastian.

"It slipped beneath the waves thousands

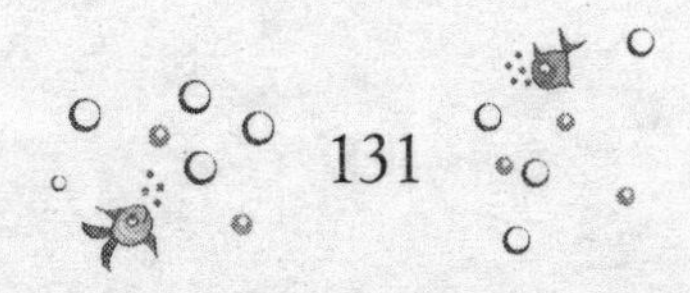

of years ago," said Zak. "Nowadays everyone refers to it as the Lost City of Tritonia, as in actual fact, if the truth be known, no one really knows where it is."

"So if no one knows where it is," retorted Maddie, "how are we expected to find it?"

"Oscar knows where it is, don't you, old son?" Zak smirked and cocked his head on one side as he glanced at his new friend. "He says he can give us directions how to get there. Isn't that right, Oscar?"

"Certainly is," said the octopus.

"Can't he take us there?" asked Maddie hopefully.

"No," Zak shook his head. "Oscar's packing his bags, says he's off before the barracudas get back – otherwise there'll be trouble."

"Where will he go?" asked Sebastian.

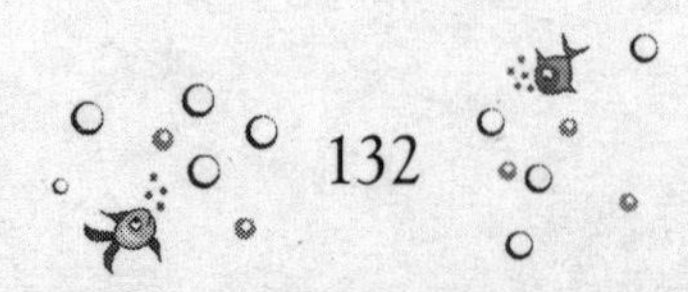

"He'll be looking for another job," said Zak. "But before then he says he's going home – to see his mum." Looking at the octopus Zak added, "Isn't that right, Oscar?"

Oscar gave a huge sigh of contentment. "Certainly is," he replied.

"Oscar says we need to get right away from here as quickly as we can," said Zak, as a little later, after taking their leave of the octopus, the friends swam away from the wreck of the *Golden Fleece*. "He said the barracudas would be home for their tea very shortly and if we weren't careful, we could find ourselves ending up on toast."

Maddie shuddered.

"They are going to miss Oscar," Zak went on. "Sounds like he's the best

security guard they've ever had. That ink he squirts keeps any intruders at bay."

"Is that what that black stuff was?" asked Sebastian in amazement.

"Yep," said Zak. "All octopi do it apparently. Wonderful device. I got him to give me some. " He lifted his head and Maddie caught sight of an oyster shell that was hanging on a throng of seaweed round his neck.

"What do you want that for?" she asked in amazement.

"Never you mind." With a cackle Zak tapped the side of his beak with the tip of one wing.

"I wonder why they took the comb to this Lost City of Tritonia," said Maddie.

"Now that we don't know," admitted Zak.

"They must have sold it to someone

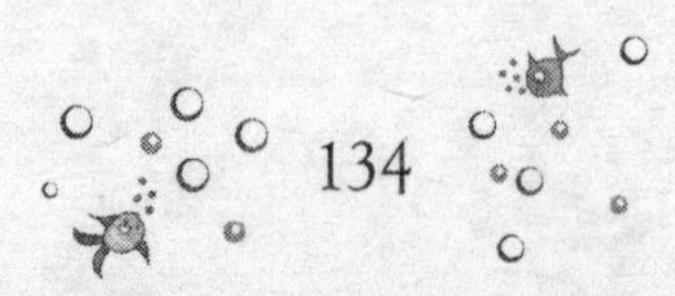

who lives there," said Maddie. "But I wonder who?"

"Lucius said collectors would be interested in buying the comb," said Zak thoughtfully. "Maybe that is who we are after."

"Maybe," Sebastian agreed. "But I think we should stop all this nattering and get on. If what your friend Oscar said is right, Zak, it sounds as if the Lost City of Tritonia is a fair old distance away, so we have some serious swimming ahead of us."

"Oh Sebastian, how much further do you think it is?" gasped Maddie. "I'm getting really tired."

It was much, much later and it seemed to Maddie as if they had been swimming for ever, through miles of coral reefs, twisting and turning through what

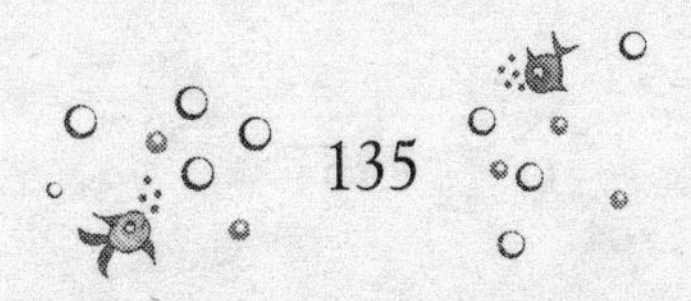

seemed like a labyrinth of narrow alleyways.

"I don't know," Sebastian admitted. "I was hoping we were going to reach Tritonia before having to stop to rest, but it doesn't look as if that is going to happen now. In fact, if I'm really honest, I've a horrible feeling we may have taken a wrong turning back there."

"You mean we're lost?" asked Maddie fearfully.

"Could be," Sebastian admitted. "I'm not really sure."

"There's a hollow over there between those rocks," said Zak. "Let's stop there for a while."

Wearily the friends swam to the hollow and sank down on to the soft sand of the seabed.

They closed their eyes, exhausted by all

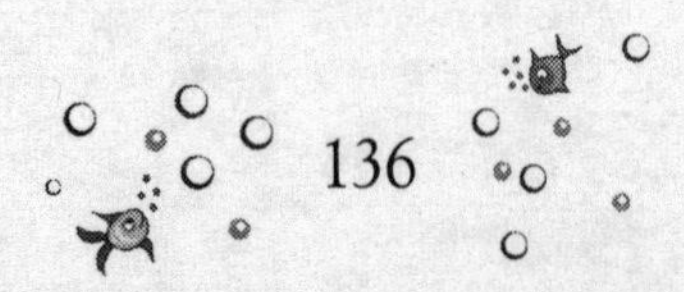

the activity, and within a very short space of time they were all fast asleep.

It was Maddie who woke first. Opening her eyes, she lay very still. Something had wakened her, but she wasn't certain what it was.

Sebastian was sound asleep on one side of her, and Zak was snoring noisily on the other. But it wasn't the sound of Zak's snores that had awoken her, it was another sound, a soft, wheezy noise which was very close by.

She continued to lie very still, afraid to move, fearful of whatever it was so close beside them that was making the strange noise. Since coming to the bed of the ocean the friends had encountered so many unusual creatures that Maddie found herself dreading just what this might be.

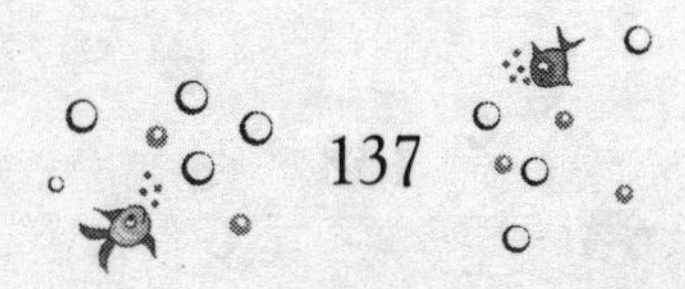

Her heart began pounding, but she knew the only way to find out what it was would be for her to move her head, very slowly, in the direction of the noise.

Before she could do so, however, the noise suddenly stopped.

Maddie held her breath, then another noise took the place of the rustling. This was a sort of twittering sound.

Maddie frowned. She knew this noise. Someone was giggling. Giggling softly, and very close by.

Swiftly, in one movement, she turned her head. The giggling stopped and she found herself staring into four startled pairs of eyes.

"Oh," said Maddie and sat up. "You are seahorses!"

The largest of the little green and white creatures tossed its head and nodded.

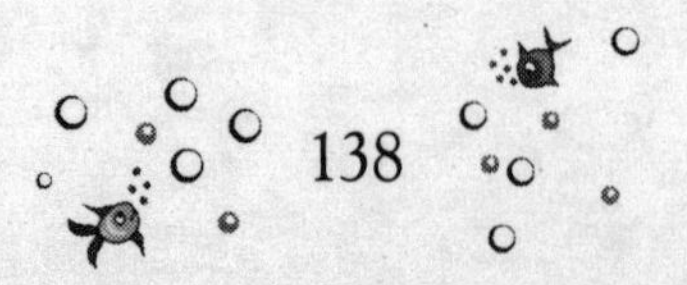

“But why are you laughing?” Maddie demanded in a loud whisper.

The smallest and prettiest of the horses began giggling helplessly again. “It’s him. . .” it gulped at last as the others joined in, holding their sides with their fins and shaking with laughter. “He looks so funny!”

Maddie turned to see what the little seahorse meant, then realized it was Zak they were laughing at. He was still snoring and at the end of each loud snore he blew out a long line of rainbow-coloured bubbles.

“Does he always do that?” asked another of the seahorses.

“I don’t know,” said Maddie, but even she was smiling now. Zak really did look very funny, lying there, flat on his back, his wings stretched out on either side and

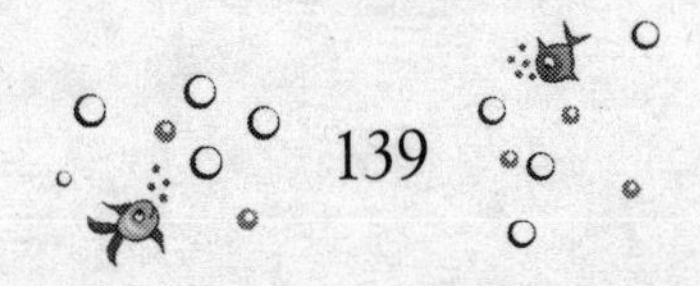

his beak pointing up in the air. "I don't think I've ever really seen him asleep before."

"Who are you?" asked the biggest of the seahorses, curious now.

"My name is Maddie," Maddie replied. "That is Sebastian," she glanced at the sleeping boy by her side, "and the noisy one there is Zak the raven."

"But you aren't creatures of the sea," said the seahorse. "Why are you here?"

"We are on our way to the Lost City of Tritonia," said Maddie then she paused as the seahorses all looked at each other. "I suppose you don't happen to know how much further we have to go, do you?" she asked anxiously.

"Actually, you are very close," said the

largest seahorse. "All you have to do is find the rusty anchor, then turn left and keep straight for a while . . . but. . ." he hesitated. "Why do you want to go there?"

"Well, it's rather a long story," said Maddie, "but we are looking for a comb."

"A comb?" said the largest seahorse, and he sounded puzzled.

Maddie nodded. "The comb was stolen from a friend of ours and we know it has been taken to the Lost City. It is our job to get it back."

"It's very dangerous in the Lost City, you know," said the seahorse.

"Oh," said Maddie. "Why is that?"

"Because of the monster," said the seahorse.

"What monster?" said Maddie uneasily. She had had quite enough of monsters for one day.

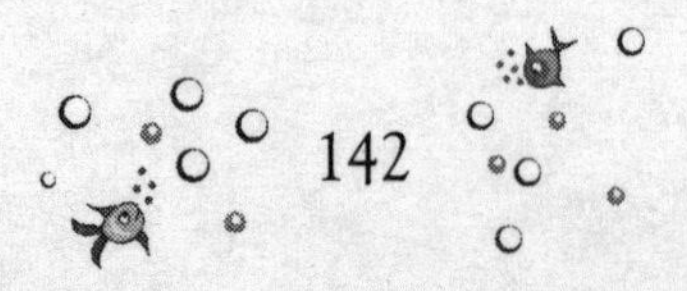

"The one who lives there," said the little seahorse.

"Oh," said Maddie. "I see." She hesitated, "So who else lives there?"

"You don't understand," said the little seahorse. "That's the whole point. No one else lives there, only the sea monster. At one time there used to be other creatures who lived there, but not now."

"It's the ugliest sea monster there ever was," said another of the seahorses. "All the other creatures who lived in the Lost City have left because they were afraid of it."

"Oh dear," said Maddie. "How dreadful."

"Do you think the sea monster has your friend's comb?" asked the little seahorse.

"Well, I suppose it must have if it's the only creature who lives there," said Maddie uneasily.

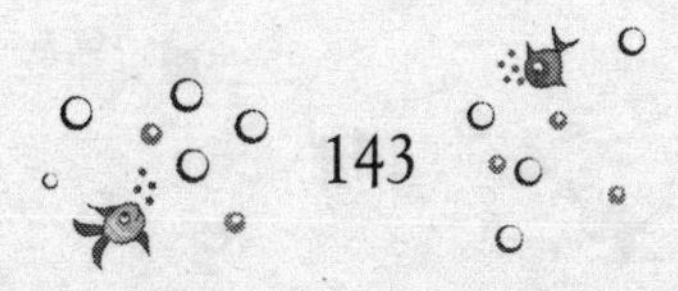

"So what will you do?" asked another seahorse.

"We'll ask the monster for it back," said Maddie. She spoke firmly, but inside she felt far from confident.

"And do you think it'll just give it to you?" asked the big seahorse in disbelief. "Just like that?"

"Well, it might," said Maddie hopefully.

"Fat chance of that. . ." said the little seahorse.

"It isn't of any use," Maddie explained patiently. "Not to anyone else. You see, our friend who owns the comb is a mermaid and it is only useful to her."

"Huh," said the big seahorse. "Try telling the monster that."

"We will," said Maddie.

"Well, rather you than me," the big seahorse replied.

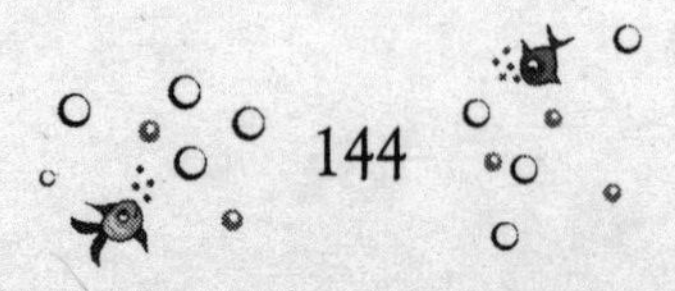

"Eh? Wassat? Wassat? Wass happening?" Zak had suddenly stopped snoring and opened his eyes. Now he was sitting bolt upright, staring at the ring of seahorses in alarm.

"It's all right, Zak," said Maddie. "These are seahorses. They have been most helpful."

"So why are they looking at me like that!" demanded Zak.

"Actually, you were snoring," Maddie explained.

"I don't snore!" protested Zak.

"Yes you do!" chorused the seahorses.

Zak looked uncomfortable, then he shrugged and said, "Yeah, well, lots of people snore. There's nothing unusual in that."

"But not everyone looks as funny as you did," said the largest seahorse, and they all

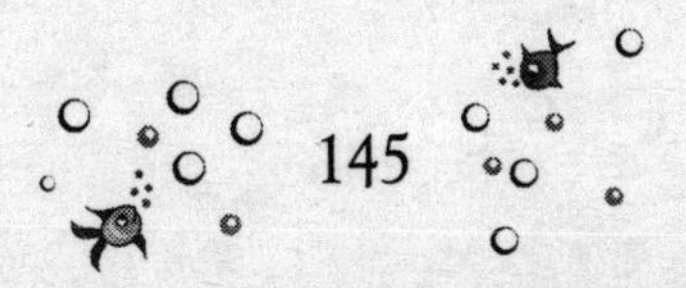

went off into fits of giggles again.

"What do you mean?" Zak glared indignantly, first at the seahorses then at Maddie, but at that moment Sebastian also awoke. Maddie hastened to tell him that they were very close to the Lost City, then went on to explain about the sea monster who lived there.

"Well, no one said it was going to be easy," said Zak, as he stretched then rubbed his eyes with one wing.

"So which way do we have to go?" asked Sebastian, scrambling to his feet.

"We'll show you," said the little seahorse. "Come on, follow us and we'll take you as far as the rusty anchor."

With that the little band of seahorses turned, and dipping and bobbing they led the way through the water in the direction of the Lost City of Tritonia.

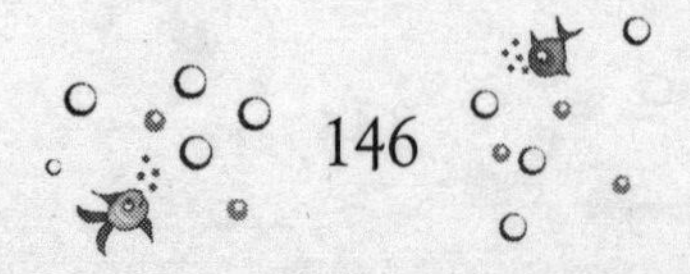

Chapter Eight

The Lost City of Tritonia

"Here it is," said the little seahorse over its shoulder. "The rusty anchor."

The huge anchor, half-embedded in the sand and covered in seaweed, was indeed rusty and looked very old.

"This is where we have to leave you," said another of the seahorses. "But you will come to Tritonia if you turn left and

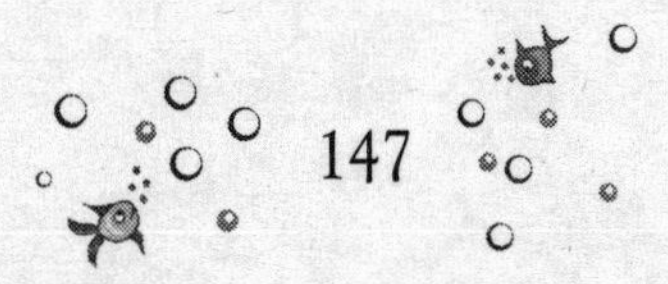

then keep swimming in a straight line."

"Thank you very much for your help," said Sebastian.

"But what about the sea monster?" asked the little seahorse anxiously.

"Sebastian has a magic spell," said Maddie proudly. "You'll use it, won't you, Sebastian?"

"If I have to, yes," Sebastian nodded. "But if we can manage without it, we will, just in case we need it to fight off barracuda attacks on the way home."

"Well, the best of luck," said the largest seahorse.

"Sounds as if we're going to need it," said Zak.

After waving goodbye to the seahorses, they swam on through more coral reefs and past tall pillars of rock.

It was Maddie who eventually noticed

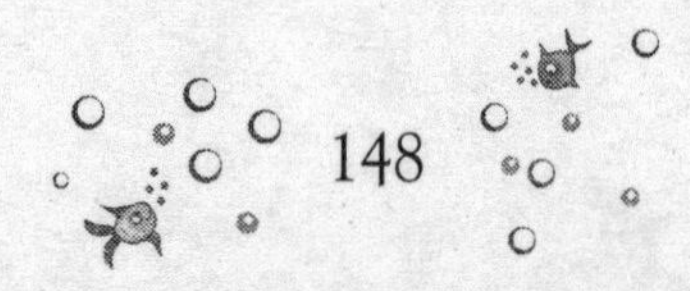

that the appearance of the pillars had changed. Instead of being rough rock they were now columns of stone with fluted surfaces and with strange faces carved into their tops.

"And look," she cried a moment later, "those are buildings over there, not rocks, and over there!" She pointed at structures that rose on either side of them out of the seabed, some tilting crazily backwards or forwards at weird angles.

"Isn't it strange," said Maddie, gazing around in awe, "to think that this was once a great city and that people lived here?"

"It still is a great city," said Zak. "It just happens to be covered in water now, that's all."

They swam on past the huge buildings, which looked as if they might once have been places of great importance like the town hall, or the official residences of high-ranking people.

"It's very quiet," said Sebastian.

"The seahorses said the monster lives here on his own now," said Maddie. "I wonder which building he lives in?"

"This one here looks like a temple of some kind," observed Zak a little later, as they approached a large, ornate building with dozens of steps leading up to a very grand entrance flanked by yet more pillars.

"It looks as if it was once a very important place," said Maddie. "Shall we go inside?"

"Might as well," said Sebastian. "We have to start somewhere."

"What if the monster just rushes out and attacks us?" asked Maddie warily.

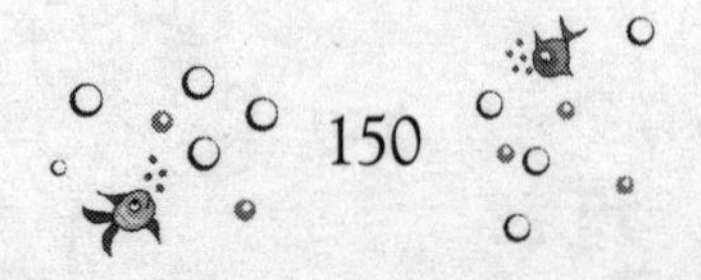

"Then I suppose we will just have to use the spell," said Sebastian.

"That is, if you can remember it," scoffed Zak.

"I can," said Maddie.

"Quiet!" commanded Sebastian suddenly.

"What?" said Zak. "What is it?"

"I thought I heard something." By this time they had swum between the pillars and had entered what seemed to be a huge entrance hall. There were yet more fluted columns that seemed to stretch for miles leading off into corridors or other large halls. Between the columns there were statues, many statues that gazed haughtily down at the friends with unseeing, stony faces.

"I can't hear anything," said Maddie gazing anxiously around.

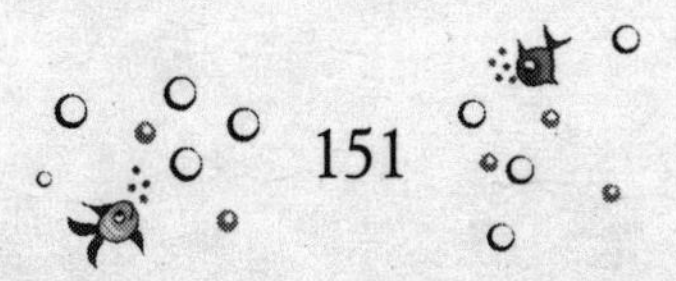

They swam on a little further, then Sebastian stopped. "There it is again!" he said. "Listen. I did hear something. Can't you hear it?" he demanded.

"Do you mean that sort of roaring noise?" said Maddie uneasily. "I did hear that, but I thought it was just the sound of the sea – like the noise you hear when you put a shell to your ear."

"If it was only that, we would have heard it before, when we were outside," said Sebastian. "No, this is something else."

"Oh jeepers!" said Zak. "Yes, I can hear it now. Sounds a bit like a hungry lion. What do you think it is?"

"I'm not sure," said Sebastian.

"Do you think it's the monster?" asked Maddie in a small voice.

"That's what I was thinking," admitted Sebastian, "but I didn't like to say."

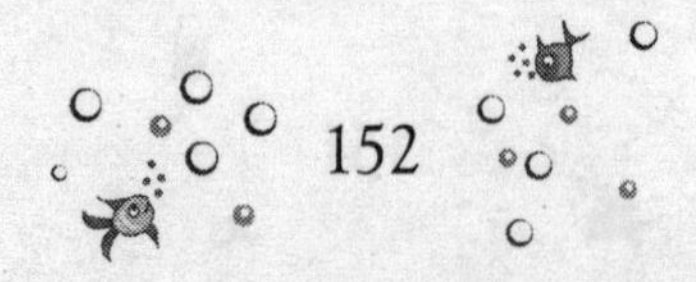

"Nothing human could make a noise like that," squawked Zak.

"That's why I didn't like to say," said Sebastian.

"What should we do?" whispered Maddie.

"We have to go on," said Sebastian. "Our mission is to retrieve the mermaid's comb and we can't do that until we find it. We know the monster has it in his possession. So let's think about this logically. Where do you think would be the obvious place for him to keep a comb?"

"On his dressing table?" said Maddie.

"Good thinking," said Sebastian. "So in that case what we have to do is to find the monster's bedroom."

"Oh boy!" Zak put his head under his wing.

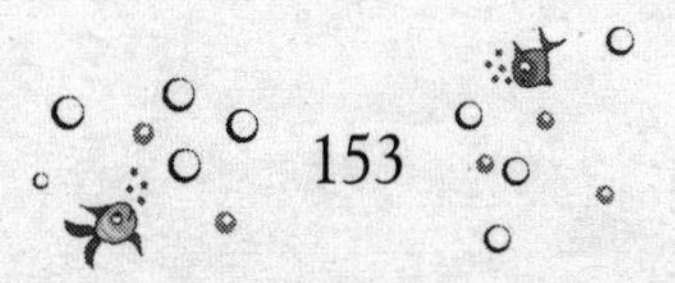

Together they moved on, this time into soaring rooms flanked by marble pillars of black, green and gold.

On and on they swam, through one room after another and, every so often, the sound of that deafening roar thundered through the marble halls and the friends would stop and clutch each other in terror until its echo died away.

"It's getting closer," said Maddie fearfully. "I'm sure it is. That last roar sounded much louder than the others."

Still fearfully, but bravely, the friends swam on. Just when Maddie was beginning to think that this place would go on for ever, they swam into yet another room, but this one was different from the others in that at one end there was a huge platform.

In the centre was a stone pallet with a

scrolled pillow of marble, whilst around the platform were enormous scallop shells open to reveal hundreds of pearls and other precious trinkets.

"Look at the size of that bed," said Zak with a muffled squawk. "I guess this must be a king-sized monster we are after."

Maddie gulped and stared at the pallet with wide eyes, but Sebastian seemed far more interested in the shells.

"I think," he said excitedly, "that those are what we need to be searching for Seraphina's comb. . . And I think we need to be quick. . ." he trailed off as another deafening roar filled the chamber and surrounding halls.

"That one was definitely closer. . ." Maddie gulped. "Much closer. . . I think. . . I think he's coming this way."

"We must hide," ordered Sebastian.

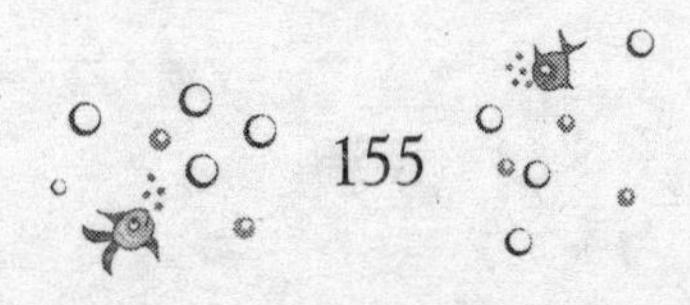

"Come on, quickly, both of you." He struck out, and leading the way, swam across the platform and behind one of the huge shells.

"No one can see us here," he said softly. "But we should be able to watch and see what happens."

As the sound of yet another roar filled the air the friends huddled together, arms and wings around each other.

A moment later Sebastian cautiously lifted his head. "It's coming," he whispered. Then he gasped. "Oh my goodness! I've never seen anything like that in my life!"

He tightened his grip on the other two, and Maddie, who by this time was shaking in terror, squeezed her eyes tightly shut.

Roar after roar filled the air as the

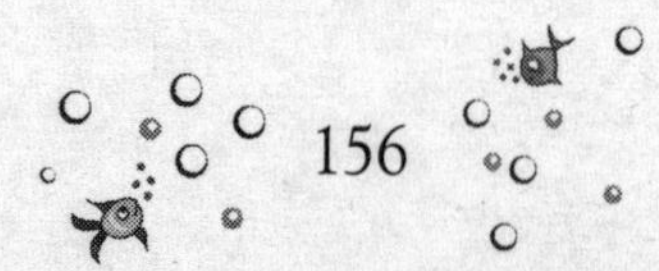

monster came through the hall between the marble pillars and approached his sleeping chamber.

"I think I would rather have st-stayed and p-played hide and seek with the barracudas," stuttered Zak. Then even he fell silent as Sebastian prodded him.

Only when the mighty roars ceased at last did Maddie allow herself to peep through her fingers and around the edge of the scallop shell. And when she did she could hardly believe what she saw.

The creature before her was indeed like no other beast she had ever seen, whether in a book or in a zoo, whether of her world or of any other.

It was big, very big, yet at the same time it appeared to be crouching. It was covered in grey scales like a fish, but had clawed feet, and wings that sprouted from

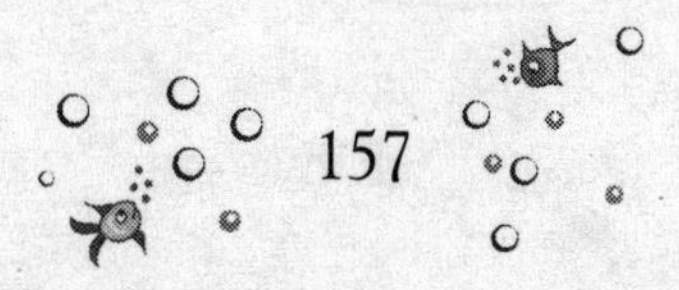

its humped back, like those of a dragon. Its head was enormous with a great mane of matted seaweed-like hair that grew

down its back and tumbled forward over its face. In the centre of its forehead was a single eye, and its mouth, which lolled

open, revealed an alarming array of black, rotting teeth.

It was so hideous, but at the same time so amazing, that just for the moment Maddie forgot to be afraid.

"It's not a fish. . ." she whispered.

"Well, it's certainly not a bird!" muttered Zak indignantly, by this time peering over Maddie's shoulder.

"Sshh!" said Sebastian warningly.

Hardly daring to breathe the friends watched as the creature lumbered on to the platform and dragged itself to one of the scallop shells.

With its claw-like hands it began scrabbling about until at last, with a flourish, it produced an object from amongst the pearls and held it aloft.

From their hiding-place the friends had no difficulty seeing what it was.

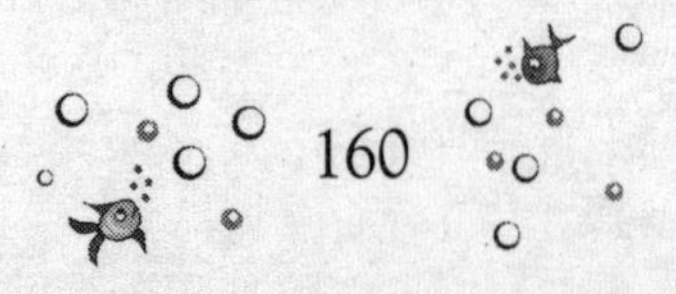

"It's the comb!" breathed Sebastian.

"What's it going to do?" said Zak. "Surely it doesn't think that will sort out that awful tangle on its head!"

"Look," breathed Maddie. "There is a mirror on the back of the shell. They watched in horror-filled fascination as the Monster peered into the mirror and began to try to comb the great matted mass of its hair.

"It won't do it," whispered Sebastian. "The comb only works for Seraphina."

"I don't think it can know that," Maddie whispered back.

"Maybe someone should tell it," hissed Zak.

"Are you volunteering?" said Sebastian.

"Not likely!" Zak shuddered, his wet feathers spiking at the very thought.

"Hopefully when it finishes, it'll go

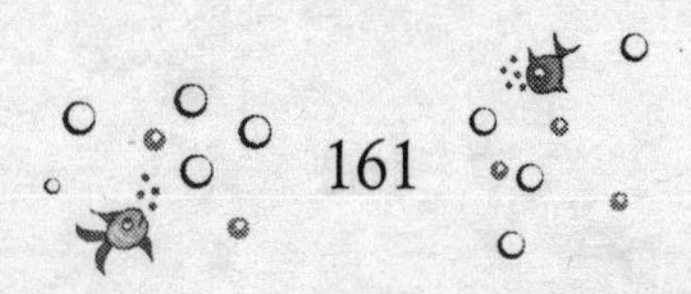

to sleep," said Sebastian. "If it does, that will be our opportunity to take the comb."

"What if it doesn't?" whispered Maddie.

"In that case we'll just have to wait," said Sebastian. "I imagine even monsters have to sleep sometime."

The monster spent a long time trying to get the teeth of the comb through the thick tangle of its hair, but the task proved to be hopeless.

"I said it wouldn't be able to do it," whispered Sebastian.

At last the monster gave a great helpless roar of frustration. To the friends' astonishment, peering at its reflection again, it said in a very loud, sad voice, "Will nothing rid me of the evil curse that makes me look this way? Am I to be alone for the rest of my days?"

With that it flung the comb back into the shell and, with a great shuddering sigh, turned and lumbered across to the stone pallet.

Maddie leaned forward round the edge of their hiding-place for a better look.

"Careful, Maddie," warned Sebastian softly. "Don't let it see you!"

"But. . ." Frowning, Maddie leaned forward a little further. "Oh!" she whispered. "Oh look, it's crying! Oh poor, poor monster!"

Sure enough, even as they watched, the monster's great shoulders began to heave and huge tears trickled from its one eye and down its face to merge with the salt water all around.

By this time Maddie was on her feet, about to rush forward and comfort the

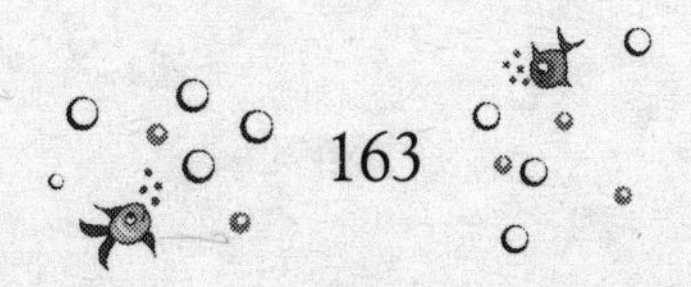

unfortunate monster, and it was only Sebastian's quick thinking that stopped her. Together, he and Zak restrained her.

"You mustn't Maddie," Sebastian said firmly. "If the monster finds us here there's no telling what it might do."

"But the poor thing . . . it's crying . . . it's so upset because it's ugly. . ."

"You heard what the seahorses said, Maddie," said Sebastian, "that all the other creatures left Tritonia because they were so afraid of the monster."

"And now it has no one," said Maddie. "It doesn't have any friends at all."

Together they watched as the monster heaved itself on to the stone pallet, where with a great sigh it lay down, then closed its one eye.

They watched in silence and Maddie found she had a big lump in her throat.

"It's asleep," said Sebastian at last as the sound of rumbling snores filled the vast room.

Together the friends tiptoed from their hiding-place and approached the platform.

"It's terrible when you hate the way you look," said Maddie, running her tongue over the brace on her teeth.

While she swam round the stone pallet looking at the great form of the sleeping monster, Sebastian swam swiftly to the open shell. With a fearful glance towards the pallet he gingerly took the comb from its bed of pearls.

"We have it," he said softly, holding the comb aloft in triumph. "We must go now and get as far away from here as we can, before the monster wakes up."

"Good idea," said Zak. "I don't fancy being around when it finds the comb is

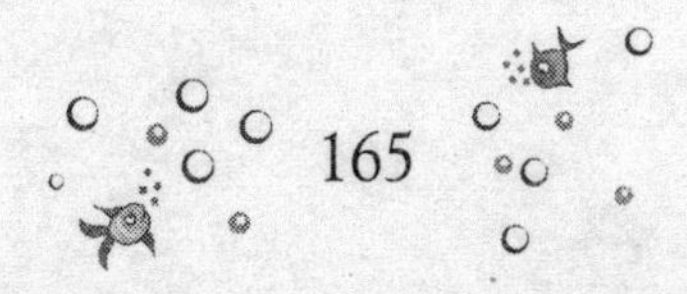

missing. Come on, Maddie."

But Maddie wasn't listening. Instead, she was still circling the stone pallet and staring curiously at the figure of the sleeping monster.

"The monster said something about a curse," she said slowly.

"Yes," Sebastian agreed, "but. . ."

"He also said something about having to spend the rest of his days alone, didn't he?"

"Something like that, I think," muttered Sebastian, "but we mustn't stop, Maddie. We need to get as far away as we can before the monster wakes up – there's no telling what it might do to us if it finds us here."

"You still have a spell," said Maddie stubbornly.

"I know," said Sebastian trying to remain patient, "but we have to keep

that. We may need it before we get back to the Crystal Caves. What if the barracudas are waiting for us? How do you think we'll get past them?"

"He's right, Maddie," said Zak. "Come on, we really do need to go now."

Sebastian and Zak began to swim away from the platform between the marble pillars, and with one last lingering look at the monster, Maddie reluctantly began to follow them.

They had swum through the many halls, and had almost reached the steps of the temple, when with a cry Maddie suddenly stopped.

"For goodness' sake!" said Zak crossly. "What is it now?"

"It's no good," she said. "I can't go on. I can't leave that poor monster. I'm going back. I'm sorry Sebastian, but if you won't

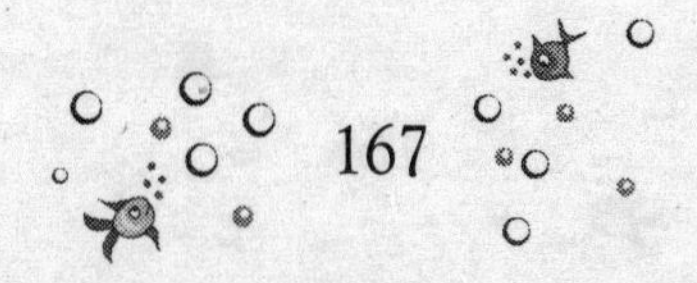

do anything for it, you'll just have to go back without me."

"Oh boy!" Zak threw his wings up in the air. "Can you imagine explaining that one to Zenith!"

Chapter Nine

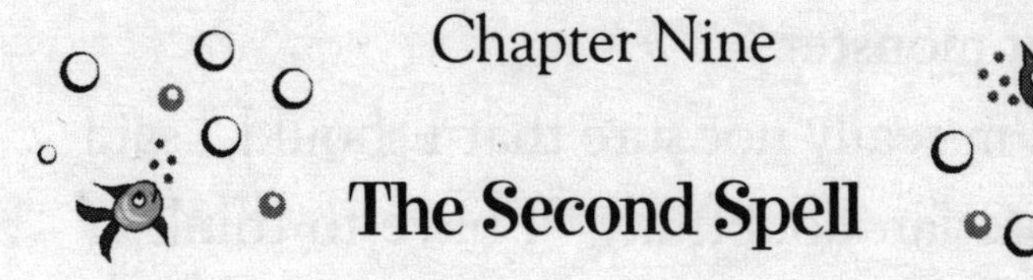

The Second Spell

"Maddie, wait!" called Sebastian, but she carried on swimming without so much as a backward glance. With a great sigh he struck out after her and moments later he was joined by a tutting, muttering Zak.

In silence the three of them swam back to the monster's bedchamber. Luckily when they got there, the monster appeared still to be asleep on the vast stone pallet that was its bed.

"So what do you want me to do?" asked Sebastian when at last he caught up with Maddie.

"I want you to use the last spell," Maddie replied, "to lift the curse on the poor monster."

"I'm really not sure that I should," said Sebastian doubtfully. "I have to think of getting us all back, and we could still find ourselves in all sorts of danger."

"And what about the monster? Does it have to stay like that, ugly and unloved for the rest of its life?" demanded Maddie hotly.

"Well, it doesn't really know any different, does it?" said Sebastian. "Not if it's always been like that."

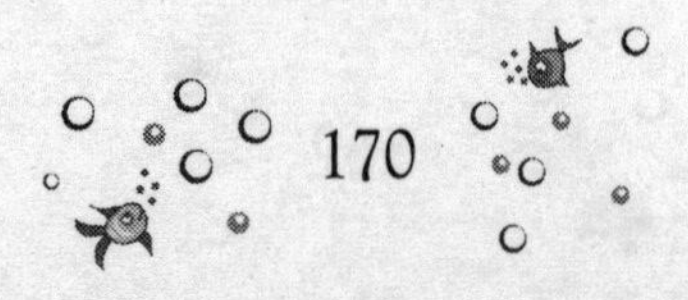

"It knows it's ugly," Maddie retorted. "It also knows everyone is scared of it because of the way it looks, and I happen to think that's terrible. Just think how you would feel Sebastian, if it was you."

Sebastian looked troubled and threw an uneasy glance at Zak.

"Zak once told me," Maddie went on, "that you were found in a basket on the steps of the East Tower when you were a baby. Just suppose someone had put a curse on you and you grew up really hideous. So hideous that everyone . . . the Princess Lyra, and the Crown Prince Frederic, and Zak and Thirza all poked fun at you. How would you have felt? That's what I'd like to know."

"She has a point, old son," said Zak. "I can't say I'd like it either. Handsome fellow like me . . . that really would have

curtailed my activities, I can tell you."

"All right! All right!" said Sebastian. "I'll use the spell, but just don't come crying to me when the barracudas are preparing to have you grilled on toast, that's all!"

But Maddie wasn't listening, instead she was looking at the monster. "Oh," she cried, "it's waking up! Quickly Sebastian, the spell, before it sees us!"

But it was too late, for the monster had opened its one eye and had already caught sight of the friends. At first it simply seemed amazed to find anyone there at all, then it stretched, before giving a mighty roar, opening its mouth wide and showing all its black, rotting teeth.

"Oh my stars!" gasped Zak. "For goodness' sake Sebastian, do something!

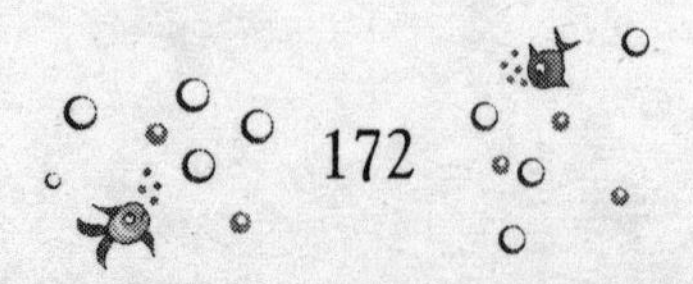

When he knows you've got the comb, we won't just be grilled on toast, we'll be swallowed whole!"

"Come on, Sebastian," said Maddie, as she stood defiantly in front of the monster. "We'll say the spell together."

"All right." Sebastian took a deep breath.

"Zambazine of Zizabar,
Zazcalooza Zazcalash.
Summon your blue magic,
In one stupendous flash!"

As they finished reciting the lines of the spell Sebastian lifted his hand, and there was a single, blinding flash as the transparent light in the underwater chamber caught the aquamarine in the ring he wore.

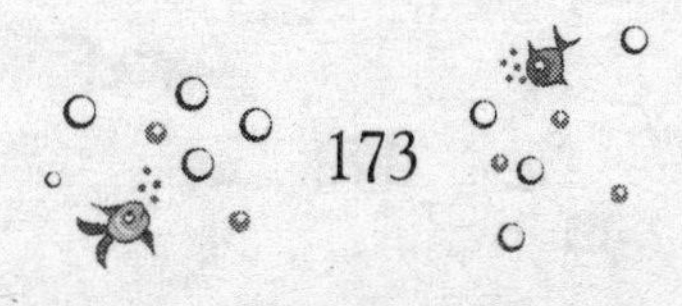

As the monster turned its great head, glared at Sebastian and began moving towards him, Sebastian said in a loud voice that only wavered slightly, "May this magic lift the curse on the monster."

There was a second flash, so bright that for a moment it seemed to blind them all, then as Maddie blinked, once, then twice, and rubbed her eyes, she saw to her dismay that the monster had stood up and was lurching towards them.

"Oh!" she gasped. "Oh Sebastian, the spell hasn't worked! It's coming after us!"

"Jeepers!" squawked Zak. "You must have got it wrong, Sebastian."

"I didn't. . ." Sebastian began.

But Zak obviously didn't intend hanging around to find out. Turning, he began flapping furiously in an attempt to get away from the monster. He was joined almost immediately by Maddie, and then by Sebastian, as with arms and wings flailing, and legs working like pistons, they began to swim for all they were worth while the roars of the monster filled the chamber and echoed in their ears.

It was Maddie who noticed it first; the silence as they reached the rows of pillars at the entrance to the chamber. She suddenly realized the monster's roaring had stopped.

Still swimming furiously, she threw a quick, fearful glance over her shoulder.

Then she looked again. And again. Then she stopped.

"Come on, Maddie!" cried Sebastian. "Hurry! We have nothing to help us now. We are on our own."

"Wait!" cried Maddie.

"Oh for goodness' sake, what now?" squawked Zak.

"I don't think we need anything to help us any more," said Maddie. "Look! Look, there's something happening to the monster!"

With that the other two turned and looked and eventually stopped swimming. Instead they too stared in astonishment at what was happening on the platform.

The monster had drawn itself up to its full height and stopped its dreadful roaring, and even as they watched, the sheer size of the creature seemed to be growing less.

Incredibly, just like a large snake, it appeared to be shedding its outer skin.

The ugly grey scales and the dragon-like wings slipped to the floor where they were joined seconds later by the thick,

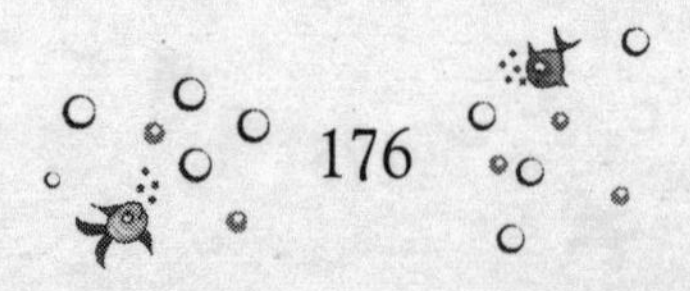

matted hair. And finally the face, the hideous face, fell like a mask. Then it was all washed away by a huge wave that crashed and foamed around the pallet, hiding the figure from the view of the watching friends.

The foam and spray eventually subsided and the friends gasped at what they saw, for where the monster had once been in all its ugliness, there now stood another figure.

This was a tall, handsome man with a halo of golden curls around his head. He also had scales, but fine silvery scales that ended in a beautiful finned tail. In a kind of wonder he gazed down at himself, then, turning, stared at his reflection in the same mirror which before had reduced him to despair.

At last, turning back again he quietly

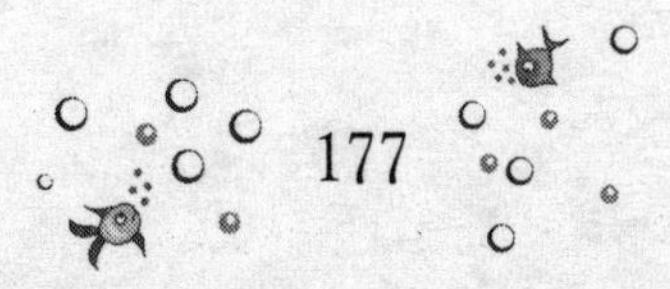

surveyed the friends and it was then that Maddie noticed that his eyes were the colour of emeralds.

"Well, bless my soul!" muttered Zak. "If it isn't a merman. Well, I never!"

"Who are you?" said the merman, the green eyes narrowing.

"I am Sebastian," said Sebastian, visibly pulling himself together as he recovered from the transformation that had just taken place before their eyes. "This is Zak the raven," he went on, "and this is Maddie. Maddie is from the Other Place," he explained. "The WishMaster, Zenith, sent us here to grant the wish of Seraphina the mermaid, who wanted her comb returned to her."

As Sebastian spoke he held up the comb. "You paid the barracudas for this comb, didn't you?" he added accusingly.

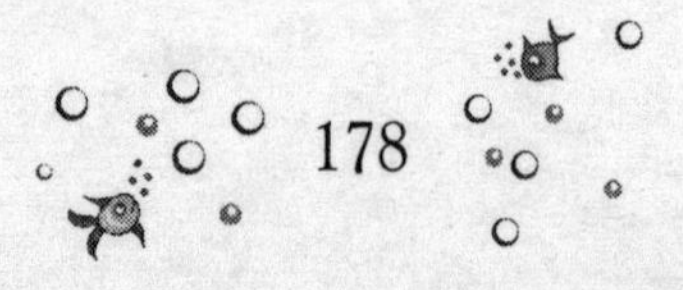

The merman frowned. "The barracudas brought the comb here," he said slowly. "They told me that a mermaid's comb had magical powers, that it could make one beautiful. And yes, I paid them for it. I paid dearly," he glanced towards the pearls in the scallop shell.

"But the comb only works for the mermaid who owns it," said Maddie.

"I was beginning to suspect something like that when it didn't work for me," said the merman.

"How come you didn't know that, if you're a merman?" asked Zak suspiciously, his head on one side.

"I didn't know that's what I was," the merman replied wonderingly, looking down at his tail. "All I knew was that I had a curse on me that made me more ugly, and more hideous, than any other monster that ever roamed the seabed."

"Do you know who could have put that dreadful curse on you?" asked Maddie.

"It was the sea serpent that I lived with until she died," said the merman slowly. "She once told me she'd made sure I would stay here with her for ever, because no one else would ever want me."

"How wicked," said Maddie with a gulp. "But it's all right now, because Sebastian used his magic to lift the curse."

"It was Maddie who persuaded me to use the spell," said Sebastian. He was still looking slightly stunned after hearing the merman's story.

"So I have you both to thank," said the merman, "for restoring me to my rightful self."

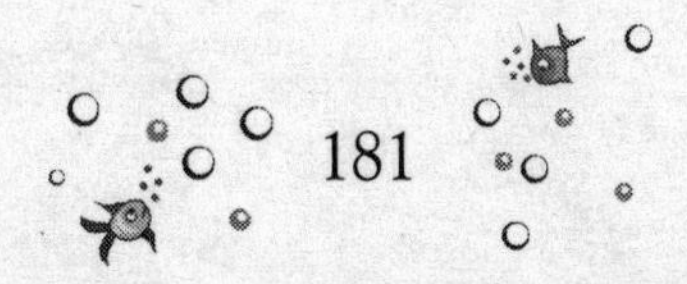

"Ahem!" coughed Zak.

"Zak helped too," said Maddie hurriedly. "He rescued us from the clutches of Oscar the octopus."

"Well, thank you all," said the merman. "Without you I would have remained as that terrible creature until the end of my days."

"What will you do now?" asked Maddie curiously. "Will you stay here?" She gazed round at the vast marble chambers of the Lost City.

"I don't know," said the merman.

"I think you should come back with us to the Crystal Caves," said Sebastian. "The caves are the home of the merfolk. I'm sure they will be delighted to see you."

"Thank you," said the merman. "I should like that. And I will also be able to

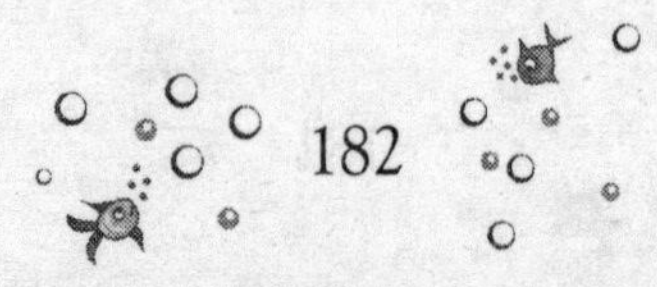

apologize to the mermaid whose comb was stolen. What did you say her name was?"

"Seraphina," Maddie replied. "And yes, I'm sure she'll be pleased to see you. . . Oh Sebastian!" she turned to him clapping her hand over her mouth. "I've just thought, do you suppose this merman is the one who was stolen from the Crystal Caves when he was a baby?"

"I would say there's a very good chance," said Sebastian. "What do you think, Zak?"

"Well, I have to say, it did cross my mind," said Zak. He turned and peered curiously at the merman. "If that is the case, old son, your name is Stephano, and when you get back to your people I'm sure you'll find that a certain young

mermaid will be very pleased to see you. Very pleased indeed!"

Together with the merman, the friends swam out of the temple and through the deserted, lonely streets until at last they left the Lost City of Tritonia far behind them.

To their delight and amazement, when they reached the rusty anchor they found the seahorses waiting for them.

"We were worried about you," said the little seahorse with a shy smile at Zak.

"Were you?" Zak puffed out his chest. "Well, I must say it was kind of you to be concerned, but, as you can see, there was no need."

"Who is this?" asked the largest seahorse, curiously eyeing the merman up and down.

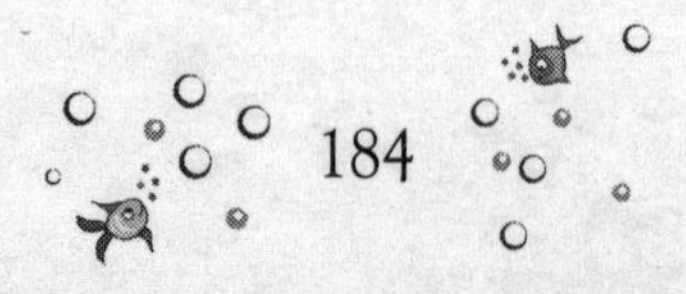

"This, believe it or not," said Sebastian, "is the dreaded sea monster that everyone was so terrified of. He had a curse on him which we've lifted, and as you can see, in reality he is a merman whom we believe was stolen from the merfolk when he was a baby."

"Were you stolen by barracudas?" asked the largest seahorse.

"More than likely," said the merman. "I gather they've been up to their evil tricks for years. I suppose they must have sold me to the sea serpent who put the curse on me."

"Talking of barracudas," said Sebastian uneasily, "we still have to get past them to get back to the Crystal Caves."

"Don't worry about that," said the largest seahorse. "We know another way back on an underwater stream which

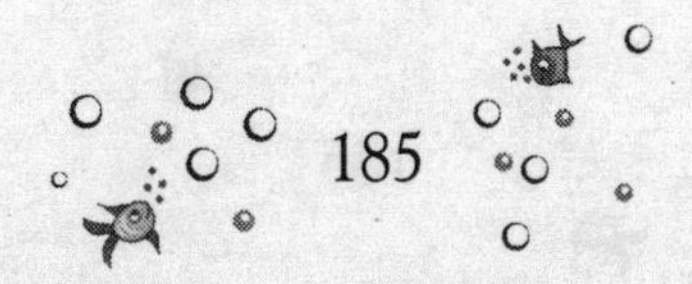

means you won't have to go anywhere near the Rainbow Lagoon. We'll show you the way."

"That's jolly decent of you, I must say," said Zak, while Sebastian gave a huge sigh of relief.

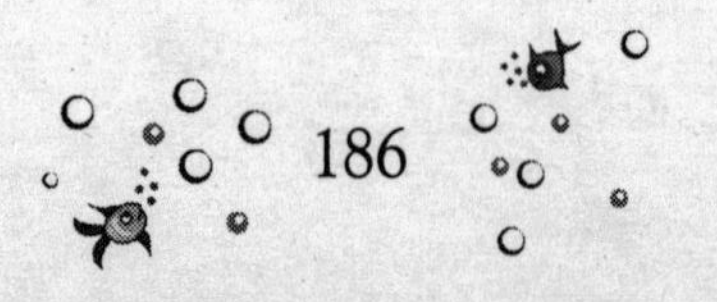

Chapter Ten

The Wish is Granted

The seahorses escorted Maddie, Sebastian, Zak and the merman along the secret underground stream that bore them effortlessly along on its strong current through a maze of rock tunnels, right back to the seabed beneath the Crystal Caves. True to their word they avoided the Rainbow Lagoon so there were no

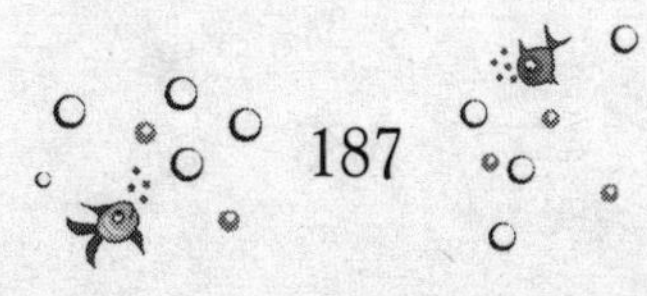

terrifying encounters with barracudas, stingrays or any other frightening creatures of the deep, but neither, of course, did they see Oscar again.

"Shame about that," said Zak. "Great chap, Oscar, I wouldn't have minded another yarn with him."

The seahorses took their leave amidst a flurry of farewells and thank yous just outside the home of Lucius the lobster.

"You will come and see us again one day, won't you?" The smallest and prettiest of the seahorses fluttered her long eyelashes at Zak.

"Course we will," said Zak gruffly. "Just try keeping us away."

"That's rich," whispered Sebastian to Maddie, "when you consider it was Zak who didn't want to come down here in the first place!"

"So you're back then?" As the seahorses formed a line and swept away, Lucius stuck his head out of the little door in his pot. "Got the comb?" he asked, suspiciously eyeing the merman up and down.

"Yes," said Sebastian. "We've got the comb."

"And that's not all," said Maddie. "We've brought this merman back with us."

"Well, I can see he's a merman," snapped Lucius crossly. Then with a sudden crack of his claws that made them all jump, he said, "Where did you find him? Who is he?"

"We believe he was stolen from here when he was a baby," said Maddie. "He was taken to the Lost City of Tritonia where a sea serpent put a curse on him

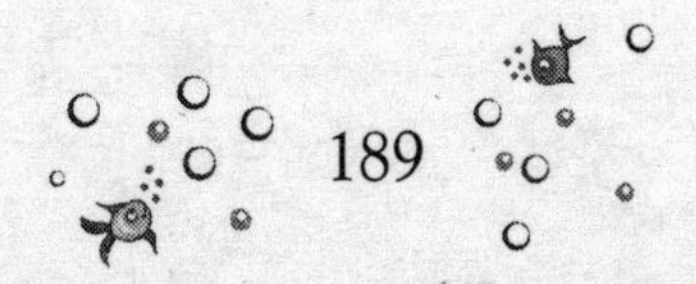

and turned him into a hideous monster. Sebastian used his magic to lift the curse."

"Oh my giddy aunt!" cried Lucius. "He must be Stephano!"

"Yes," said Maddie excitedly. "That's what we thought as well."

"Terrible to-do there was at the time you went missing," said Lucius peering up at the merman. "My word!" he went on after a moment. "There'll be some celebrations up there tonight, and no mistake. Might just come along myself."

"What about your rheumatism?" asked Zak slyly.

"Oh, it's better today. Much better." With a little grunt of glee Lucius rubbed his claws together, then he turned and crawled back into his pot, shutting the door behind him.

Sebastian looked up through the deep

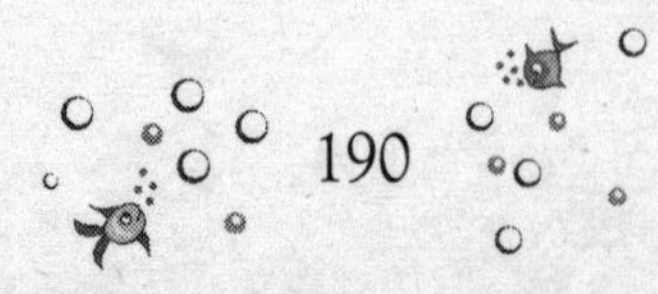

green of the water. "Come on," he said to the others. "This is where we need to surface. Is everybody ready?"

"Yes." They all nodded and as Sebastian gave a count of three they struck outwards and upwards. It seemed only moments later that they had left that strange world of colours and shapes behind, and were surfacing in the turquoise waters of the pool in Seraphina's cave.

Silvio, who must have seen a disturbance in the waters and guessed it was them, was waiting anxiously at the side of the pool.

"Oh!" he cried, as one by one they broke through the surface of the water. "You're back! Oh, thank goodness! I was beginning to fear you might be too late."

"What do you mean?" gasped Maddie as

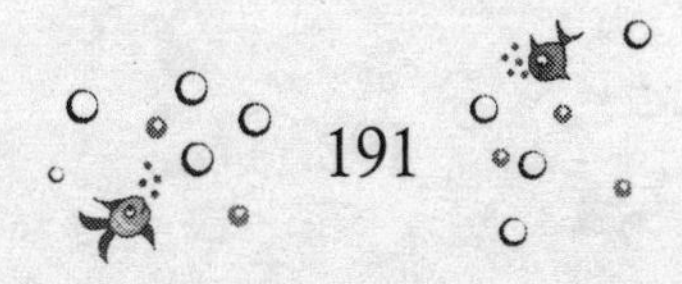

she shook the water from her red curls.

"Seraphina is very ill," said Silvio. "Only her comb can save her now." He looked desperately from one to the other of them, his gaze flickering curiously over Stephano, then back to Sebastian again. "Do you have it?" he said.

"Yes," said Sebastian. "We have the comb."

Silvio gave a great sigh of relief while Maddie looked round the cave, peering into the alcoves, which appeared to be empty. "Where is Seraphina?" she said anxiously.

"She's moved into another, deeper cave," said Silvio. "She feared you wouldn't be able to get the comb so she's gone there to die."

"Oh dear!" wailed Maddie. "Quickly Sebastian, the comb!"

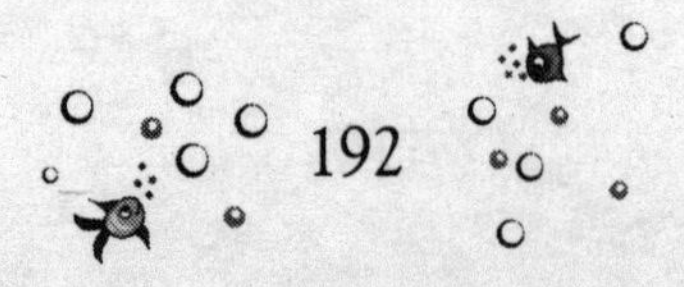

From inside his turquoise garment Sebastian took the comb and was about to hand it over when the little merboy stopped him.

"You bring it," he said to Sebastian. "That's only right. You got it back for her so you should be the ones to give it to her."

Sebastian hesitated, glancing at the others.

"Go on," said Zak suddenly. "You and Maddie go. Stephano and I will wait here.'

With a flash of his tail Silvio beckoned to the two friends to follow him, then he dived into the water and began to swim towards the waterfall that cascaded into the pool.

It was cool and dark behind the curtain of water and very noisy, so noisy it was impossible to talk to each other, so instead

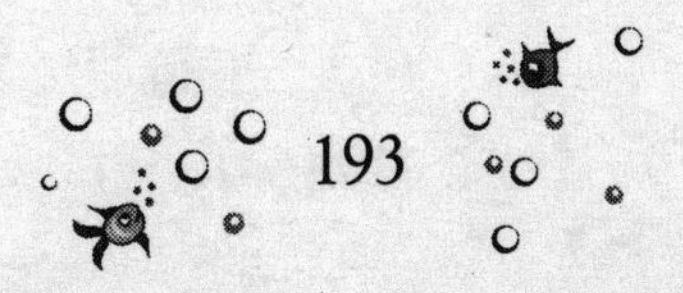

they just followed the little merboy as he swam further and further down a narrow stream into another cave.

And at last he stopped, turning towards the friends as they swam to join him. There beside him, on a shelf of rock, was Seraphina. She was so weak she could barely lift her head in greeting.

"Oh Seraphina," whispered Maddie as she hoisted herself out of the water. "We're here now, don't worry, we have your comb."

"My comb. . .?" Seraphina's voice was so faint they could barely hear her. Maddie turned to Sebastian who handed her the comb, then crouching down beside the mermaid she began to attempt to comb out the hopelessly matted tangle of her hair.

At first she thought her task would

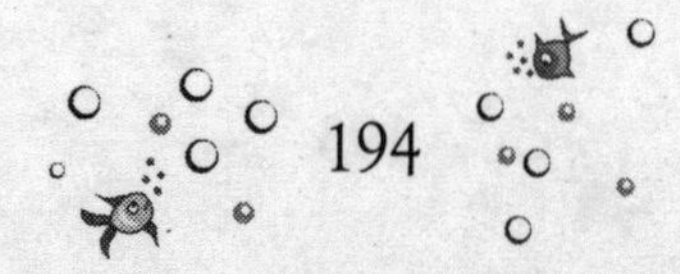

prove to be impossible, but gradually, to her amazement, it became easier and easier, just as if the golden tresses automatically responded to the teeth of the comb.

Carefully she teased out the thick tangles until in the end the comb skimmed effortlessly, faster and faster through the mass of waves and curls that tumbled over the mermaid's shoulders.

By now Seraphina was crying tears of relief, happiness and joy that fell into the water around her.

"Oh, how can I ever thank you enough," she cried. "My dear, dear friends. Without your help I would not have lived for very much longer."

"We have a surprise for you," said Maddie, when at last Seraphina's hair had been restored to all its former glory,

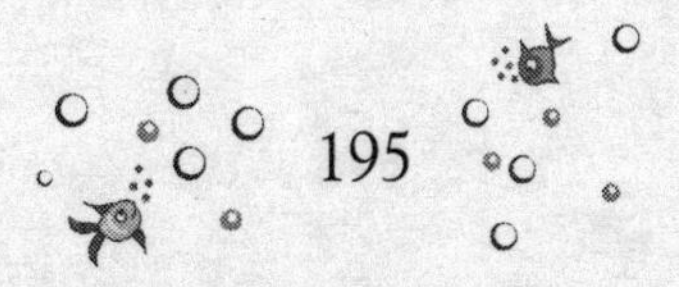

and her scales shone and glittered again.

“A surprise?” The mermaid lifted her head and looked from Maddie to Sebastian, then back to Maddie.

“Yes,” it was Sebastian who answered, Sebastian who had been sitting on the edge of the water, watching with quiet satisfaction as Maddie had combed the mermaid’s hair. “Remember you told us of the merbaby, Stephano, who had been stolen from here many years ago?”

“Yes,” Seraphina nodded.

“Well, we believe we have found him,” said Sebastian triumphantly.

“You have found him?” Seraphina looked bewildered. “You have found the merbaby?”

“Yes,” said Maddie excitedly, “only he isn’t a baby now, of course, he’s a merman.”

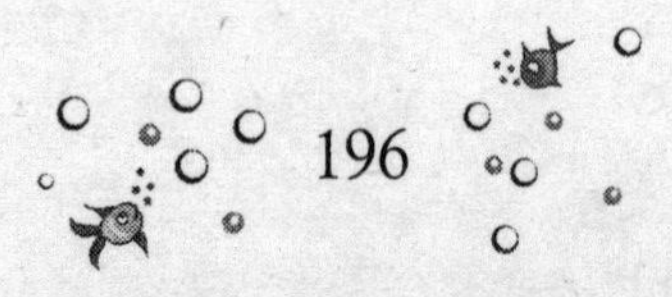

"We thought he must be dead after all this time," said Seraphina wonderingly. "When he didn't come back to me. . ."

"He couldn't." Maddie hastened to explain. "He'd been turned into a hideous monster by a wicked curse. He didn't even know he was really a merman. Sebastian lifted the curse with his magic," she added proudly.

"How wonderful," whispered Seraphina. "So . . . so where is he? Where is he now?"

"He's outside in the cavern." It was Silvio who replied. "He looks nice, Seraphina, really nice."

"Are you ready to come and meet him?" asked Maddie.

"Oh yes, yes, of course," said Seraphina. Then looking down at herself she said anxiously, "Do I look all right?"

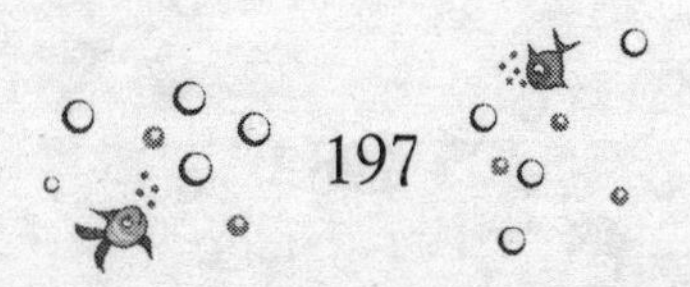

"You look beautiful," said Maddie. "Absolutely beautiful."

"Come on then," said Sebastian, slipping into the water again.

"Wait," said Seraphina suddenly. "There is something we need if we are to meet Stephano." She turned to the merboy. "Silvio?" she said.

"Yes, of course," the merboy turned and swam into another cave, returning a moment later with something in his hand.

"What is it?" asked Maddie curiously.

"Stephano's comb," said Seraphina simply. "It's been here waiting for him since he was a baby. Without it he too will wither and die."

Maddie, Sebastian and Silvio escorted Seraphina, swimming beside her as they entered the cavern and approached Stephano and Zak who waited there for

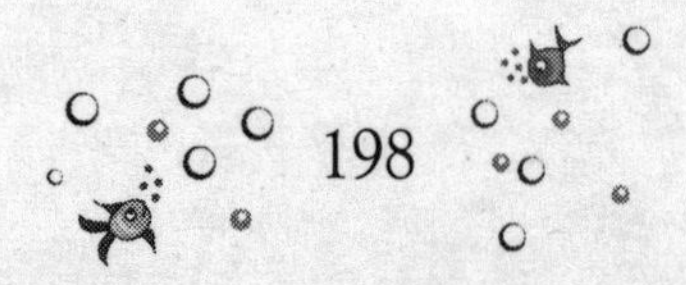

them on the rocks around the turquoise pool.

Afterwards Maddie thought she would never forget that moment as long as she lived. The moment when Seraphina and Stephano were reunited, when emerald gaze met emerald gaze, when their fingers touched and when at last they embraced.

Even Zak was overcome and had to keep wiping his eyes with his wing.

While the mercouple talked, catching up on all that had happened, and Stephano used the comb that Seraphina gave to him, drawing it effortlessly through his locks of golden hair, Silvio went off to fetch the friends' clothing, and refreshment for them after their journey.

"So the mermaid's wish is granted and our task is over," said Sebastian with a

sigh, and there was a touch of sadness in his voice. "We'll have something to eat, then it's time for us to go back to Zavania and report to Zenith."

When Silvio returned, accompanied by other merfolk all anxious to meet the long-lost Stephano, he bore the mother-of-pearl salver just as he had before, and once again it was piled high with exotic-looking fruits.

Maddie was quite sorry to change out of the catsuit she had worn for her underwater adventure. Her school uniform seemed very dull in comparison. When she emerged from the alcove she found the others tucking into the fruit while Seraphina was telling them yet again how much she owed them.

"Is there nothing we can do for you in return?" she asked anxiously.

"No, of course not," Sebastian began, but he was cut short by Zak who began hopping up and down.

"Actually," he said, "there might be something. . ." Although Sebastian turned and glared at him, he calmly went on, "I've been thinking. . . It seems to me you're going to have to be a little more careful around here in future. You can't go on living the rest of your lives in fear of those pesky barracudas."

"I was thinking the same thing," said Stephano. Then drawing himself up proudly, he said, "But now I am home, I hope I will be able to help protect my people from their cowardly attacks."

"Very commendable, I'm sure," said Zak. "But it seems to me you need a little more than good intentions to thwart those evil varmints."

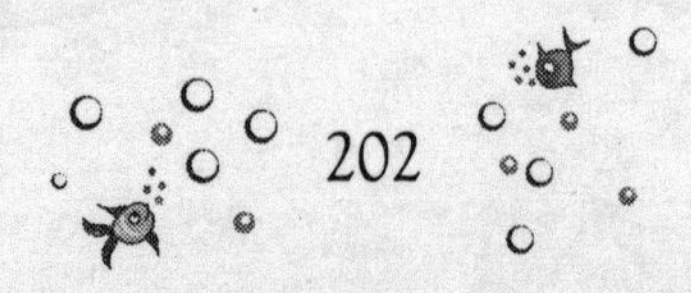

Stephano frowned. "Did you have something in mind?"

"Yes," said Zak. "I have." He paused, then when he was sure he had everyone's attention, he went on, "What you need here is a good security guard, and believe it or not, I just happen to know the ideal guy for the job. He's big, he's clever and he's reliable; but most important of all, he knows the barracudas probably better than anyone else. I also happen to know that he's out of work at the moment and will be looking for another job."

"That sounds just what we need," said Stephano. "Who is he?"

"His name is Oscar," Zak replied.

"And where can we find him?"

"Ask Lucius," said Zak. "I'm sure he'll be able to tell you where Oscar's mum lives."

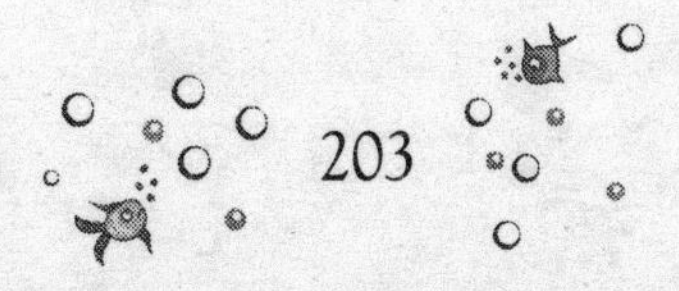

"All that remains now," said Sebastian, "is for us to say goodbye."

"You can't go yet," said Stephano firmly. "Seraphina and I want you to attend our wedding."

"When will it take place?" asked Sebastian a little anxiously.

"Immediately," Stephano replied. "We've spent enough time apart as it is."

"In that case," said Sebastian, "we'll be delighted to accept."

"Oh yes," breathed Maddie.

"That," said Maddie, "was quite the most beautiful wedding I ever saw." With a deep sigh of pure satisfaction she stopped waving to the merfolk who had all lined the rocks around the Crystal Caves to say farewell, and leant back against the cushions in Sebastian's boat.

The two dolphins, Delphine and Demetrius, had been waiting for them at the mouth of the caves, and as the friends had settled themselves in the boat they had once again taken the tow-rope in their mouths.

"I hope we can return one day," said Maddie as the dolphins towed them across the sparkling blue waters of the bay, and the merfolk gradually became no more than tiny dots in the distance. "They were such lovely people, and it was all so romantic."

"That was a stroke of genius from you, Zak, suggesting Oscar as their security guard," said Sebastian.

"I'm not just a pretty face, old son, as I keep reminding you," said Zak.

It seemed in no time at all they were back at the mouth of the river and the

dolphins had said goodbye and returned across the bay, leaping through the waves laughing and calling to each other.

"Well," said Sebastian as he began to guide the boat up river, "that seems to be the end of our underwater mission. All that remains now is for us to report to Zenith and see if he approves of all we did."

"Could be dodgy, that," said Zak, who had perched himself at the back of the boat. "Wonder what he'll make of us using one of his precious spells for turning a monster into a merman."

They needn't have worried, because after they'd returned to the East Tower and been fussed over by Thirza, who had been getting worried about them, they climbed the stairs to the turret room to find that

Zenith had just perfected another spell and was actually in a very good mood.

"Come along," he boomed, gazing down at them. "I want to know everything that has happened."

"Everything?" said Zak uneasily.

"Everything," replied the WishMaster firmly.

"Well, I suppose really," said Sebastian taking a deep breath, "it all began after the dolphins had taken us across the bay to the Crystal Caves and I realized we were going to need to be able to breathe underwater. . ."

"He *was* pleased, wasn't he?" said Maddie dreamily as she lay amongst the cushions in the bottom of the boat. It was much later and Sebastian and Zak were taking her home.

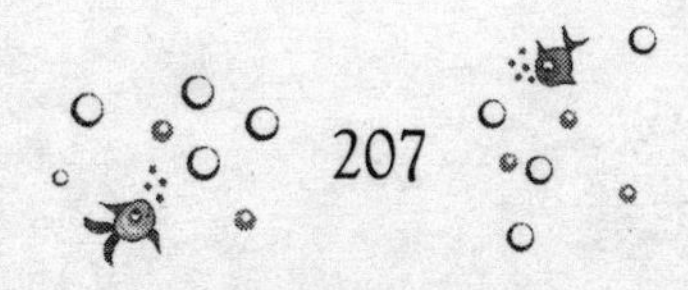

"Yes," Sebastian leant on the pole for a moment and considered, "I do believe he was."

"He certainly used some long words," cackled Zak. "Compassionate, shrewd, courageous. . . At this rate, Sebastian, you'll soon have those Golden Spurs."

"Oh not too soon, I hope," said Maddie before she could stop herself. "Once you are a fully-fledged Wishmaster, Sebastian, you won't want me any more. Unless of course you'll still need me to help you remember the spells."

"And the rest," cackled Zak.

They drifted on downstream and as Maddie saw the outline of the willows amongst the mist her heart grew heavy because she knew then that were nearly home.

"I think," said Sebastian, and even his

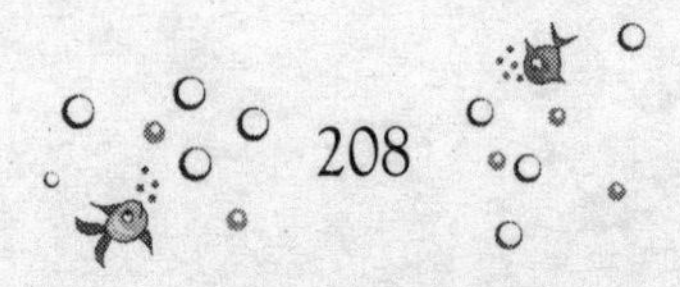

voice sounded a little husky now, "you'll find that you are home at the exact time you should be."

"I don't really want to go home," said Maddie, staring at Sebastian. "I'd much rather stay here with you. And you, Zak," she added hastily as the raven indignantly flapped his wings. "But I have to go. I'm supposed to be going to a party at my school. I don't really want to go because that awful Jessica Coatsworth will be there."

"Don't go then," said Zak. "I must say I didn't like the sound of her."

Maddie sighed. "I have to go," she said. "My friend Lucy will be expecting me to go, so I can't really let her down.'

She hesitated as Sebastian slid the boat in under the willows against the riverbank. "You will come back?" she said anxiously, as he stepped out of the boat then turned and held out his hand to help her ashore.

"Of course I will," he said softly. "Just try stopping me. As soon as someone else makes a wish, I'll be back."

"Goodbye, Sebastian," Maddie whispered as he continued to hold on to her hand, just a little longer than was really necessary. "Goodbye, Zak."

"Goodbye, Maddie."

She stood on the bank blinking furiously to stop the tears that had sprung to her eyes. The boat slid from her sight, and her last glimpse was of Zak as he turned his head and closed one eye in a huge wink.

She just had time to change from her school uniform into her turquoise top and skirt. Suddenly she didn't mind wearing

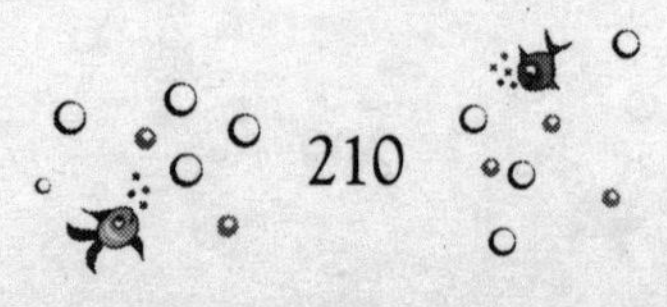

it, because it was the exact colour of the suit she had worn for her journey to the bottom of the sea.

After collecting the sandwiches and fairy cakes that her mother had made, Maddie hurried to the corner of the road only to find that Lucy had gone. She was quite out of breath by the time she arrived at school.

Lucy ran out to meet her. "Oh, there you are, Maddie," she cried. "I thought you weren't coming. I say," she went on excitedly, and Maddie could tell she was bursting to tell her something, "you'll never guess what's happened to Jessica Coatsworth."

"No, what?" Maddie wasn't really interested. Whatever had happened to Jessica Coatsworth couldn't be as exciting as what had happened to her.

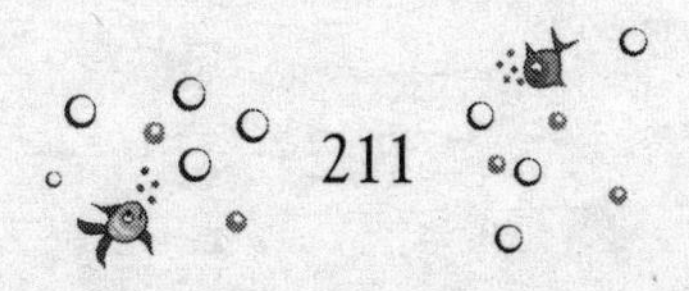

"Well," Lucy hardly seemed able to contain herself, "you know she was going on about her new outfit all afternoon?"

"You mean the 'new cropped top and gold satin leggings'?" said Maddie in a perfect imitation of Jessica's voice.

"That's right." Lucy giggled. "Well, it seems the most extraordinary thing happened on her way here."

"What was that?" Suddenly Maddie was curious.

"Someone squirted awful black ink all over her."

Maddie stopped and stared at Lucy. "Ink?" she said faintly.

"Well, that's certainly what it looked like," said Lucy. "I saw her, she was absolutely covered in it. It was in her hair . . . everywhere really. She's had to go home. Looks like it could take ages to

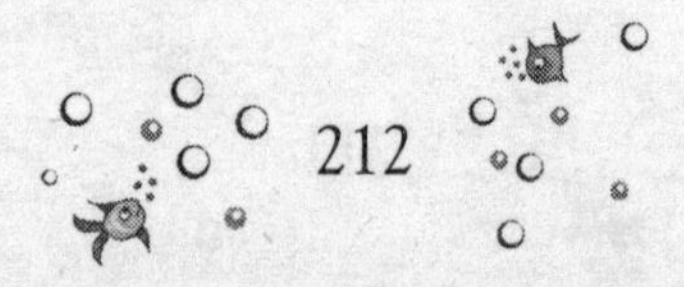

wash it all out. She'll miss the party. . ."

"Er . . . does she know who exactly it was who squirted her with this ink?" asked Maddie as she tried to ignore the unbelievable possibility that was beginning to form in her mind.

"Not really," said Lucy. "She said whoever or whatever it was seemed to come out of nowhere. One thing she did remember was seeing a large black bird. But it couldn't have been a bird. Not with ink."

Not giving Maddie a chance to say anything Lucy rushed on. "She also said she heard laughing, a loud, cackling sort of laugh, and that definitely couldn't have been a bird."

"Really?" said Maddie weakly. "How amazing. I wonder whatever it could have been."

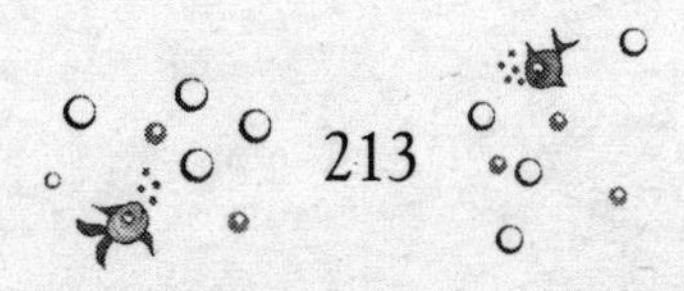

"Goodness knows," said Lucy. "I suppose really we should feel sorry for poor Jessica, but every time I think about it, I can't stop laughing. She looked so funny, and everyone saw her, even Josh Bates – you know how she goes on about him – well, he laughed louder than anyone."

They walked into school and Lucy went on, "I can't help feeling that really it serves her right. Maybe now she won't be quite so beastly. Especially to you, Maddie. Let's face it, she really was horrible to you."

"Yes," Maddie agreed. "She was."

Fighting to hide her laughter Maddie followed Lucy into school and, to her surprise, she found she was suddenly quite looking forward to the party after all.

In the magical land of Zavania, a proud princess has made a wish...

The spoilt Princess Lyra has made a wish for her brother to come home – and insists on accompanying Maddie, Sebastian and Zak on their mission to find him.

As the trail leads from a city built on water to the sinister Mountain of Sun, it looks like the prince has got mixed up in something dangerous. Can the friends overcome their differences in time to save the day?